STEPHA[...]

First published in 1995 by Nexus
352 Vauxhall Bridge Road
London SW1V 2SA

Reprinted 1995, 1997

Copyright © Stephanie Dupont 1995

ISBN 0 352 52976 5

A catalogue record for this book is available from the British
Library

Typeset by TW Typesetting, Plymouth, Devon
Printed and bound in Great Britain by
BPCC Hazells Ltd

This book is sold subject to the condition that it shall not, by
way of trade or otherwise, be lent, resold, hired out or
otherwise circulated without the publisher's prior written
consent in any form of binding or cover other than that in
which it is published and without a similar condition
including this condition being imposed on the subsequent
purchaser.

This book is a work of fiction.
In real life make sure you practise safe sex.

First published in Great Britain in 1992 by
Nexus
332 Ladbroke Grove
London W10 5AH

Reprinted 1992, 1994, 1995

Copyright © Susanna Hughes 1992

ISBN 0 352 328 25 8

A catalogue record for this title is available from the British Library

Typeset by TW Typesetting, Plymouth, Devon
Printed and bound in Great Britain by
BPC Paperbacks Ltd

This book is sold subject to the condition that it shall not, by way of trade or otherwise, be lent, resold, hired out, or otherwise circulated without the publisher's prior written consent in any form of binding or cover other than that in which it is published and without a similar condition including this condition being imposed on the subsequent purchaser.

Chapter One

Stephanie answered the phone with reluctance. Another minute and she would have been across the office and on her way home. She was tired. It had been a long day collating the latest market research on a new product range and she was desperate to get home, have a long bath and an early night. But her sense of conscientiousness would not allow her to walk away leaving the phone to ring.

'Stephanie Curtis?' The voice was cool, precise and very feminine. It was not a voice Stephanie recognised.

'Yes?'

'I'm Mr Devlin's driver. I have the car outside. He wondered if you might like a lift home.'

Stephanie's mind was racing. Devlin! She hadn't seen or heard from him for three months. She couldn't say she'd forgotten him – Devlin was not a man forgotten easily – but this message came out of the blue. Any misgivings she might have had were overcome immediately by the thought of not having to fight her way home on the tube.

'That would be very nice.'

'I'm parked outside. You'll recognise the car, won't you?'

She headed across the open-plan office too wrapped up in her own thoughts to acknowledge the goodnights of the two girls who remained. Stephanie had always attracted a lot of attention with the men in the office. Her long black hair, brandy eyes, fleshy mouth and her trim waist, complementing her firm breasts and long, lithe legs, made her an obvious target for male lust and fantasy. It was no surprise, then, when Dennis Andrews, a founder member of the lust brigade, leered at her in the lift all the way down the six floors to the foyer.

'Out on the raze tonight then, is it?' he drawled.

'No, Dennis. An early night.'

'I bet. Tucked up in bed ...' He tried to make tuck sound like fuck.

'Give it a rest, Dennis.'

'You know I'll do anything you say, Stephanie. Given half a chance.'

'Don't tempt me.' Meaning she'd like to tell him to jump into a very large vat of boiling oil.

'Why not? You tempt me.'

Dennis held the main entrance door open for her. Parked outside the building on double yellow lines was a large Mercedes coupé so clean and highly polished that the building was perfectly reflected in every panel of the car. Standing by the passenger door was a tall, slim woman wearing a black suit and white blouse. The skirt of the suit was short and revealed most of her long, shapely legs. She wore black high heels, as shiny as the car, which accentuated her pinched ankles. Her blouse was tight, more like a leotard, and clearly revealed the outline of her large breasts, flattened slightly by the material. The suit was clearly meant to be a uniform, but a very expensive one.

As Stephanie walked towards the car, and the driver opened the passenger door for her, she could see it was empty. She had expected Devlin to be there, sitting in the car waiting for her. His absence made the invitation even more mysterious.

Dennis Andrews followed in Stephanie's wake, his mouth wide open. 'Goodnight then,' he said, perhaps hoping for a lift.

Stephanie got in without replying. The driver closed the passenger door behind her and looked at Dennis.

'Goodnight, sir,' she said, turning to walk around to the driver's door. Dennis's mouth remained open as the car pulled effortlessly into the traffic.

'The office bore,' Stephanie explained.

'There's always one.' The woman drove precisely, with the minimum of effort. Stephanie remembered the way the car felt, silent, with not the slightest vibration – instantly soothing despite the snarling traffic outside. 'My name's Venetia.' She had obviously been given Stephanie's address, as she appeared not to be waiting for directions.

Stephanie relaxed into the big leather seat of the car, determined to appear cool. She watched Venetia drive. The skirt of the uniform had ridden up to display all of her thighs. She was wearing black tights, very sheer and shiny, and Stephanie could see her muscles flex in her right leg as it dabbed on the brake pedal or darted to the accelerator. The left leg remained passive. They were magnificent legs and Stephanie had to admit that Venetia had the body and the face to match.

'How long have you been working for Mr Devlin?'

'A year.'

'Where is he?'

'I'm not sure. He phoned and asked me to give you this.' Venetia reached over to the glove compartment and flicked it open. The light inside revealed a thick white envelope attached to a stem of orchids. Stephanie took the orchids out. They were a wonderful combination of yellow and white with a slash of crimson.

'They're beautiful.'

'Home grown.'

'Really?'

'Not by Devlin. But his gardener's very keen.'

'Must have a big greenhouse.'

'No, they're flown in.' She volunteered no further information and Stephanie didn't ask.

The envelope was not sealed. Inside it was a handwritten note. 'I've been thinking about you, my dear. A lot. Please accept this invitation. *Devlin*.' Stephanie searched the envelope but there was nothing else with the card.

'Is that it?'

'No. The rest is in the boot.'

'What rest?'

'You'll see.' Venetia said it with a smile, her tongue darting between her lips. There was clearly no point in enquiring further.

The rest of the journey was spent in silence. The car was so quiet Stephanie could hear the rasp of nylon against nylon as Venetia moved her legs to drive the car. Stephanie rested her head on the head restraint of the seat and closed her eyes. She remembered the night with Devlin, his huge ugly features, his banana-sized fingers, his cock, gnarled and veined, so big she had not been able to fit it all into her cunt. A shiver of pleasure ran through her body as she thought of him and that night and what he had done to her. She opened her eyes and looked at Venetia. What was her relationship with her employer? She could not believe, looking at her as she drove, that it did not involve sex.

She directed Venetia to her front door. The power-steering made the parking easy. Before Stephanie realised what was happening Venetia was out of the car and opening the passenger door. It gave her a strange feeling to be waited on like this but it was not a feeling she disliked.

Venetia opened the boot of the car. Inside was a large

leather suitcase. Stephanie recognised it from an advert in Harper's – Louis Vuitton, sculpted leather.

'I'll take it up for you.' It was not a question. Venetia took the case out of the boot and followed Stephanie to her front door. The case was obviously heavy but she carried it without apparent effort even up the flight of stairs to Stephanie's first-floor flat.

'Now you can open it.' Inside she lay the case on Stephanie's dining table and handed her the keys in a little suede pouch. She was obviously acting under strict instructions.

Stephanie did not want to appear over anxious. 'Would you like a drink?'

'Yes, some wine would be nice,' Venetia said without hesitating, almost as though this were part of the instructions, too.

'Red or white? The white is better.'

'White then. May I sit down?'

'Of course.'

Stephanie went into the kitchen. Fortunately she always kept a bottle of Chablis in the fridge. She opened it absent-mindedly, wondering what on earth Devlin had planned for her.

She handed Venetia the glass and took a sip from her own. Then she unlocked the suitcase. Venetia did not look up as Stephanie flipped the lid back. She knew what was inside or so it appeared.

The case was full of clothes. On top two swimsuits, one a practical two-piece, the other a glamorous creation of spangles and lurex that could never be exposed to water. There were two silk evening dresses, cut to reveal more than they covered, a day dress of fine cotton, three pairs of shoes, and a mass of underwear, suspender belts, matching French knickers, bikini briefs, soft and underwired bras. Three sets in all, all silk, all in the most perfect taste – classy and elegant – and all, Stephanie knew, expensive. Everything in the case was by a top designer, everything the right size, everything the right style for her.

'Did you choose these?'

'No, Devlin always chooses.' Venetia's response begged the question. She dropped the 'Mister'. And what did she mean by 'always'? He did this all the time?

'I can't accept this.'

As she said it she saw a map tucked into one of the satin pockets of the case. It was a map of Italy with a thick felt-penned circle around Lake Trasimeno.

'Devlin wanted to make sure you have everything you need. It's hot there at this time of the year.' Under the circle was scrawled in the same handwriting as the note in the car: 'Friday at six till Monday at nine.'

'I'm to pick you up at the office.'

'To go to Italy for the weekend?' Stephanie knew she had not managed to keep the incredulity out of her voice.

'In Devlin's plane. We'll be there by nine, traffic control permitting.'

'I need another drink.' What Stephanie actually needed was time to think. She went into the kitchen and closed the door behind her. Venetia said nothing and remained sitting passively on the sofa.

Stephanie knew Devlin was rich but she had no idea he had this sort of wealth. Private planes, suitcases full of clothes that probably cost as much as she earned in a year, leggy chauffeuses. She knew Devlin had wanted her sexually but she had not imagined she had made this kind of an impact on him. Or perhaps she hadn't. Perhaps this was just a regular event in his life, a rich man's game. Some men collected cars, or antique furniture: Devlin collected women. Had them delivered to him on a metaphorical plate.

As this thought occurred to her Stephanie knew it did

not matter. She didn't mind if she was one of ten, one of a hundred. She felt flattered, she felt special, and that was quite enough for her. She also had to admit that sexually the thought of Devlin was exciting.

She walked back into the living room. 'I accept,' she said simply, looking into Venetia's eyes for any reaction.

'Good,' she said without the slightest flicker of interest.

'Have you been to this lake?'

'Yes.'

'Sounds exotic.'

'It's a castle. Used to belong to one of the Italian noble families. It even has its own vineyard. Devlin's done a lot of work on it. It's very comfortable. Very secluded.' Suddenly Venetia smiled. 'Very thrilling.'

Of course it was thrilling to be flown to a castle on a lake in Italy but Stephanie knew at once that was not what Venetia meant. The word 'thrilling' seemed to hang in the air between them. She looked again at Venetia sitting back on the sofa, calm and confident, her legs crossed. Venetia met her eyes and for a long moment they looked at each other. Venetia slowly and deliberately uncrossed her legs. Stephanie watched as she did so. The black skirt covered nothing and Stephanie was sure she could see through the sheer nylon, under the seam that ran up between her legs, a thatch of pubic hair. Venetia parted her legs slightly as if to give Stephanie a better view.

'Devlin was right. You are a beautiful woman,' Venetia said, making no effort to recross her legs.

'So are you.' Stephanie could feel her heart racing, her breathing getting shallow. Venetia knew where her eyes were fixed, knew it and liked it. Months before Stephanie had had sex with a woman for the first time. It had brought her to new heights of sexual awareness but, strangely perhaps, she had not repeated the experience since then, nor had she wanted to. Until now.

'Do you mind if I take off my jacket?' Venetia said as if reading Stephanie's mind. She stood up and peeled off the black jacket of her suit. Her white blouse was cut to reveal her arms and shoulders and in profile Stephanie could see the sides of her breasts straining to escape the tight garment. Without asking or hesitating Venetia pulled the blouse over her head. She stood in front of Stephanie, feet apart, her large breasts still quivering with the movement, a challenge in her eyes.

Stephanie stood up and touched Venetia's cheek with the back of her hand. She was wearing a shirtwaister dress buttoned down the front and Venetia responded to the touch by undoing the three buttons of the dress above the waist. She slipped her hand inside the dress, found the top of Stephanie's bra and moved her hand until her fingers rested on Stephanie's nipple. She squeezed it quite hard and Stephanie moaned. In a moment Stephanie knew Venetia was going to kiss her, kiss her full on the mouth and embrace her. The idea made Stephanie flush with excitement.

Venetia had unbuttoned the dress completely now and eased it off Stephanie's shoulders, letting it fall to the floor. Stephanie made no attempt to stop it. She stood in bra, knickers and tights, her underwear practical white cotton.

'Where's the bedroom?'

Stephanie nodded towards the bedroom door. Venetia picked up her blouse and jacket and walked through the door, shutting it after her.

Stephanie looked at the table, the suitcase and all the clothes strewn around. Almost without thinking she stripped off her cotton underwear and tights. In the case she had seen a dark blue teddy in the finest silk. She stepped into it and pulled it up over her body. The crotch-piece was unbuttoned and she bent to do it up. As she found the poppers her fingers touched against the lips of her cunt

She could feel her heat. She dipped a finger between the lips and was not at all surprised to find a thick wetness there.

She glanced at herself in the mirror, transformed now by the expensive teddy. Cut high on the hips, low on the breasts, it clung to her body, making her look somehow more naked than nakedness itself. She remembered the last time she had been with a woman. Though the circumstances were very different, the excitement she felt was the same. Last time Martin had been there. Now, as she walked into the bedroom, she was on her own.

Venetia was naked lying on the bedsheet, the counterpane stripped back. Up until now her fair hair had been tightly held in the chignon at the back of her head. Now it was free, long and flowing, looking blonder than it had before. Her pubic hair was blonde too, but very sparse, and her labia were clearly exposed as she lay, legs sprawled open.

Stephanie sat on the side of the bed. Immediately Venetia pulled her down, falling on top of her like a hungry wolf eager to eat its prey. Her tongue pushed into Stephanie's mouth while her hand groped for her breast under the blue silk. Stephanie responded, kissing Venetia back hard, squirming against her mouth as she sent her hand first to find Venetia's breast, then moved it down to her cunt. Her fingers ran through the wispy pubic hair to find Venetia's hard clitoris. Venetia moaned as Stephanie's finger found the target and pushed and pulled on the delicate knob of flesh, but she did not break away from the kiss. Instead she drove her tongue deeper into Stephanie's mouth, while her hand pinched at the erect nipple under the teddy.

Stephanie had found a rhythm now. She pressed Venetia's clitoris hard against the pubic bone, then pulled it upwards, then down again. She loved the feeling of touching clitoris and cunt, of feeling a soft yielding body pressed next to her own. Venetia's grip on her nipple relaxed and she broke away from the kiss, hugging Stephanie instead as she concentrated on her own passion. Stephanie worked harder, faster as she felt Venetia's body contract around her, felt all her muscles and nerve centre on that little knot of feeling which she was manipulating. Venetia was moaning continuously now, almost forming words ('Do it, do it, do it') until finally her whole body arched up from the bed and she screamed as her orgasm crashed through her body.

Venetia did not wait for her orgasm to subside. Her hand went down between Stephanie's legs, clawing at the poppers of the teddy. She tore them free but did not wait while Stephanie started to pull the garment off; instead she plunged her head down into the thick black hair of Stephanie's crotch and found her clitoris with her hot tongue. As soon as she was free of the teddy Stephanie lay back on the bed again feeling Venetia's tongue probing her cunt. It left her clitoris and licked all the way down to her arse. For a second it flicked the rosebud of her arse, pushing for admittance, before moving up to her cunt and inserting itself there, as far in as it would go. Then back to the clitoris again, licking it hard, licking it like an ice cream. Back down again, down to her arse, this time getting into it a fraction, then cunt, then clitoris again, the complete cycle. It was driving Stephanie wild. She had never had a man do this to her.

Venetia was kneeling beside her and Stephanie opened her eyes to watch this beautiful woman's body as it worked on her. Her long hair bobbed and weaved as her head moved, her long legs tucked under her, the roundness of her buttocks curving into the long arch of her strong slim back.

Venetia concentrated on the clitoris now, licking and

flicking at it alternately with her tongue. At the same time she plunged, hard and fast, two fingers into the depths of Stephanie's cunt, making Stephanie moan. The fingers went in and out like a cock, establishing a pattern with the movement of the tongue. Stephanie felt her orgasm beginning, the first signs were always the same, like the first notes of a symphony known by heart. She knew it would build, rise, rest on a plateau, rise again and finally swamp her. She knew she could hold it back deliciously for a while, holding it at bay with some little mental trick, though enjoying the pleasure of it being there. Then she would give in to it as she did now. Take all the mental brakes off and let it pick up full speed until it careered downhill out of control, until it destroyed any sensation but itself.

Stephanie sat up and pulled Venetia up too. She took her cheeks between her hands and kissed her mouth; not just kissed but licked it, licked up all her own juices, savouring them like some expensive delicacy. Venetia did not stop her. She let her lick around her mouth as well as in it. Venetia liked to do this too. It was exciting to taste yourself on the mouth of another. Her chance would come.

As if reading her mind Stephanie broke away from Venetia's mouth and trailed the kiss down her body until she reached her breasts. She took one nipple in her hand and the other in her mouth. She sucked it, squeezed it hard between her teeth, pulled it away from the breast with her teeth, imitating each action of her mouth on one breast with her hand on the other. Each bite, each tug, made Venetia let out a little cry of mock pain. She let herself slide back to lay on the bed. Then Stephanie left her breasts and licked her navel. She looked down at Venetia's sparsely haired pubis, only inches away now. It was only the second time Stephanie had ever touched or licked another woman. She was still excited, still hot, still wet and still breathing in the way only sexual fever can induce. Her lips were on Venetia's nether lips now. At first she kissed them just as though they were a mouth, darting her tongue out between her lips to find the clitoris, then back in again as though experimenting with a French kiss for the first time. Then she probed deeper with her tongue trying to get it deep into Venetia's cunt.

As she did this she felt Venetia pulling at her ankle, so she would open her legs and allow Venetia to get her face under her body and up between her legs. She cooperated in the movement until she suddenly felt Venetia's hot mouth clamp itself on to her still wet cunt.

They were the perfect combination, in perfect harmony. Every movement of tongue on clitoris, tongue on cunt, mirrored and matched. Stephanie moved her mouth to bite playfully on Venetia's thigh; Venetia did the same. They could feel each other perfectly. They could feel their erect nipples pressed against each other's navels; their soft, smooth flesh so close the two bodies seemed to become one. Venetia's orgasm started first, making her pant for breath as she tried to keep her mouth locked on Stephanie's cunt despite the waves of feeling coursing through her. And this extra heat from Venetia's mouth made Stephanie come too, making their breath harder and hotter, setting up a chain reaction as they came together, feeling the other's orgasm as much as each felt her own, a shattering double orgasm wrenching through every nerve, every sense of body and mind.

Venetia rolled Stephanie over and kissed her mouth, determined not to miss that pleasure. Her juices tasted sweet on the mouth of this stranger, on the mouth of Devlin's woman. The thought of Devlin sent a shudder through Venetia. It was a shudder of pleasure certainly but there was an element of pain too. She had not been told what Stephanie meant to Devlin or what their relationship had been. But she knew what was going to happen now, knew it better than anyone. She had been through it herself. Through it and out the other side. An experience she would never forget. Now she was Devlin's faithful messenger, performing her tasks to the letter as she was obliged to do. Now it was Stephanie's turn.

Chapter Two

At precisely ten minutes to six on Friday the telephone on Stephanie's desk rang. The receptionist, obviously highly amused by the situation, judging by her suppressed giggles, informed Stephanie that a car was waiting for her. Stephanie picked up the case, which had been standing by her desk all day attracting admiring comments from those in the know, and headed downstairs. The last hour had seemed interminable. Now at last she was off.

Outside a surprise awaited her. Parked in front of the building was not the Mercedes coupé but one of the largest black stretch Cadillacs Stephanie had ever seen. Standing by the passenger door was not the trim figure of Venetia, but a tall, powerful-looking man in grey chauffeur's uniform and cap. As she approached he took the case from her hand and opened the large rear door to the car.

'Good evening, madam,' he said formally.

'Good evening.' Stephanie got into the huge interior of the Cadillac and settled down into the deep leather seat. The chauffeur, having deposited the case in the boot, got into the car and immediately pressed a control button to wind up the division between the passenger compartment and the driver. Obviously talking to the driver was not to be encouraged.

In the back Stephanie looked around the car. It had everything. Built into a panel on each side of the backseat were controls for radio, air conditioning, windows and electric seat adjustment. On one side, at the back of the driver's seat, was a built-in cocktail cabinet, and on the other, a unit containing a television and video recorder – all this in highly polished walnut. There was a telephone mounted on each side of the car. The carpet was deep-pile pure wool. The suspension of the car matched the interior comfort; it seemed to glide over the road as though suspended on a cushion of air.

Suddenly the television came to life and she saw the video recorder begin to turn too. A picture appeared on the set. It was Devlin.

'Sorry I can't be with you in person. Business, I'm afraid. But I'll be waiting for you at the lake. I'm so glad you could join me. Enjoy the champagne.' The picture went blank and the recorder and television were turned off, presumably by the driver.

Stephanie saw that there was a well at the side of the cocktail cabinet which held a silver wine cooler with a bottle of Louis Roederer Crystal champagne and a champagne flute all swathed in ice. Well, she thought, might as well enjoy myself. She popped the cork and poured herself a glass. Then she sat back, sipped at the delicious wine and watched the people of the street fighting their way home. She could see them perfectly through the windows of the car but they could not see her as the windows were blacked out on the outside. Occasionally at a traffic light she would see some curious passer-by trying to look in to see who on earth the big car contained. A film star, a politician, a tennis player? Stephanie sat back in the plush seat and enjoyed it. This was certainly a new experience.

She was wearing Devlin's clothes. The practical cotton dress, ideal for travel – designed by Yves Saint Laurent, she had seen on the label. And the luxurious cream silk underwear – a soft-cup bra, bikini knickers and a suspender belt. She was wearing very sheer cream stockings. As there had been no tights in the suitcase she imagined Devlin had a preference for stockings and given what was happening to her at the moment she was only too happy to oblige. In fact she had packed almost nothing of her own. Venetia had been right: the case contained every prerequisite for a weekend, right down to a toothbrush. Devlin had thought of everything. She had packed a little jewellery. There had been none in the case, for which she was grateful. That would have been too much. And yesterday she had gone shopping and purchased something she hoped Devlin would appreciate.

So where was Venetia? Stephanie had expected her to be there tonight to pick her up. She had to admit she was disappointed not to see her. Finding the control in the side panel by the seat she pressed the button to wind down the window between her and the driver.

'Where's Mr Devlin's chauffeur?'

'I'm Mr Devlin's chauffeur, madam,' he replied frostily.

'Where's Venetia, then?' she persisted.

'I don't know, madam.'

Stephanie hesitated, questions crowding into her mind. But she decided she would play Devlin's game, and pressed the control button in the opposite direction, watching as the glass panel whirred back up into position.

Would Venetia be at the lake? Or was it just going to be Devlin? If she was absolutely honest with herself, she didn't really care. If Devlin's intentions had been to sweep her off her feet, make her careless of what was going to happen to her, he had succeeded completely. In her affair with Martin she had allowed herself to be taken to new levels of sexual awareness. Whether this weekend with Devlin would produce equally new experiences she had no idea. But her affair with Martin had taught her to be open-minded and not to shy away from the unknown. She sipped at the vintage champagne, then refilled her glass. One thing was for sure: this was definitely the way to travel.

The car pulled through the gates of a private airfield. Stephanie watched as it drove up to a series of prefabricated buildings. The chauffeur stopped the car and came round to open the passenger door.

'You'll need your passport, madam,' he said. A uniformed officer had come out of one of the buildings, clipboard in hand. He quickly examined the passport Stephanie produced, made a note on his clipboard, and smiled.

'All in order. Have a good trip, miss,' he said, handing her back the passport.

Back in the Cadillac the chauffeur drove around the buildings to a line of hangars. Parked outside one of them was a white Learjet, obviously being readied for take-off, its landing steps extended from the passenger compartment. The chauffeur drove right up to the steps. From the plane a Malaysian woman wearing a tight, white rough silk Kheong-Sam high to the neck but split to well above the knee, came down. Her thick black hair was cut short and parted in the middle, a style which perfectly suited her found face and green jade eyes. She opened the car door for Stephanie.

'Good evening, madam. I'm Susie, your flight attendant this evening.' She smiled. The chauffeur had taken the suitcase from the boot and put it aboard the plane.

'Have a good flight, madam,' he said touching his hand to his cap in what passed for a salute.

'Thank you.'

'This way, madam,' Susie said, leading the way up the steps and into the main cabin of the plane.

If the inside of the Cadillac had been luxurious, the inside of the plane was palatial. In the main cabin there was a cocktail bar, comfortable sofas, leather armchairs and a dining table with four chairs, all upholstered in the finest materials – wild silk, the softest leather, burr walnut.

'We will be taking off in four minutes, madam. If you would please choose your seat and fasten your seat belt.'

Stephanie chose one of the leather chairs. She could hear the noise of the engines increase but the interior of the cabin was still remarkably quiet.

'Can I get you a drink before take off?'

Stephanie refused. She had already drunk most of the bottle of champagne on the drive and did not wish to arrive in Italy the worse for wear. That is not what Devlin would want. But she did order Perrier, which was brought at once in a tall glass with ice and lemon. Then Susie disappeared into the forward cabin.

Stephanie felt the plane moving and moments later, with no queueing for runway slots as in a commercial airport, the engines roared and they were airborne, turning immediately to head south, the whole of London spread out beneath them.

Susie returned as soon as the plane had leveled out. 'It is perfectly all right to remove your seat belt now, madam.'

'How long is the flight?'

'One hour and ten minutes.'

'Am I the only passenger?' For a second Stephanie saw that Susie hesitated before answering the question.

'Some cargo,' she said, not looking Stephanie in the eyes. After showing her the call buttons should there be anything she required, she disappeared into the forward cabin again.

Intrigued at Susie's response, Stephanie roamed the cabin enjoying the feeling of being able to walk freely about in a plane. She looked out the windows on the other side of the cabin. It was still light outside and she could pick out details of buildings on the ground below. Her feeling of excitement had not decreased since the moment she had stepped into the car. She had never been in a private plane before. It was quite an experience, she decided, something she could easily get used to.

At the end of the main cabin was a door in the bulkhead. Ever-curious, Stephanie tried it and found it was locked. But there on the floor in front of the door was a small brass key.

Stephanie picked it up and fitted it into the lock of the door. For a second she hesitated. If it were locked it must be locked for a reason. Then curiosity overcame caution – as it so often had with her – and she turned the key and opened the door.

The cabin beyond was dark. From the light flooding in from the main cabin it appeared to be an empty space stacked with a few wooden crates.

Stephanie found a switch and lights came on. Then she saw why Susie had hesitated.

There was another passenger.

On the bulkhead wall next to the door a man was strapped. He was spreadeagled against the wall and fastened to it with heavily padded leather straps at his wrists and ankles. He was completely naked, but his face was covered with what looked like a carnival mask. It had small holes behind which Stephanie could see the man's blue eyes moving rapidly, trying to see what was going on, but there was no mouthpiece and as she looked closer she could see that behind the mask a gag was strapped tightly into the man's mouth.

For a moment she thought she'd better leave, turn the lights off again and go back to the main cabin: pretend she had never seen the 'cargo'. But the feelings this apparition had aroused in her were too strong. It was like a magnet pulling her forward, impossible to resist.

The man's body was good, well muscled and firm. Closing the door Stephanie stood in front of him, looking into his eyes through the small holes in the mask. As she did his penis stirred. He was getting an erection. Tentatively at first she ran her hand down his chest as far as his waist, then up again. There was nothing he could do to stop her. She could do anything she wanted with him. The idea made her feel instantly hot. She could feel her cunt beginning to cream, or was that her imagination? She circled the man's cock lightly with her hand and it sprung to full erection. The man moaned through the gag. It sounded as though he was trying to say 'please' but she could not tell for sure. She trailed her other hand across his chest again, then pinched at one of his nipples. He moaned again. She pinched alternatively and saw his penis swell each time she did so.

She could feel her knickers clinging to her now, hot and damp. It was not her imagination. She hitched up her skirt and pulled her knickers down over her stockings. The man's eyes tried to follow her movements as far as his restricted vision would allow. Stephanie's excitement was beginning to supersede any other feeling. She did not care what happened. No doubt the champagne she had consumed emboldened her. This whole trip was so bizarre, so extraordinary she could only follow her instincts. There would be time for regret later. Now she wanted an orgasm. She wanted to take this man.

Kneeling in front of the man she used her hand on her clitoris, then pushed two fingers into her cunt. There was no resistance. The feelings of excitement she had experienced in her mind had been perfectly communicated to her body and her cunt was already wet. As she was only inches from it anyway, she opened her mouth and sucked his cock in, producing another, louder moan. His cock was hot and very hard. She ran her tongue around the tip then took her mouth away and licked instead his big hairy balls.

This was like a fantasy, like the games she'd played with Martin. The helpless man, his cock hard and available for her pleasure. Her fingers weren't big enough to satisfy her. She needed cock in her, his cock. Pulling her skirt up over her waist she held his cock in one hand down between her legs and pushed her backside into his navel. It was not the ideal position but it would just work. She guided the cock between the lips of her cunt then bent forward to increase the angle. Yes, it was beginning to push between her labia and into her. She could feel all her juices running over him. She pushed back further and then he was home, a good few inches into her, and she gasped at his heat. It was as though his cock were on fire. She started to fuck him by pushing her backside up and down on him while she wanked her clitoris. He was moaning regularly now what sounded like 'thank you, thank you.'

'*No!*' Susie stood in the doorway. '*You must not.*' With a strength that belied her fragile appearance she pushed Stephanie forward and off the man's cock.

'How dare you!' Stephanie was furious at the interruption.

'He's on punishment. It is not allowed.'

Stephanie stared into the cold, angry eyes of the Malaysian woman. For a second neither woman moved.

'I want him.'

'It is not allowed for him to come.' Stephanie was too aroused and too excited to leave it at that. Then she realised she had a trump card to play.

'Devlin told you I was to have everything I wanted, didn't he?'

'Yes.' A look of uncertainty entered Susie's eyes.

'Yes, *madam.*' Stephanie corrected.

'Yes, madam,' Susie repeated obediently.

'Everything I wanted?'

'Yes, madam, but ...'

'I am telling you I want this. Now.' Without waiting for a response Stephanie pulled off her dress. She reached behind her back to unclip her bra, then stopped. She was beginning to realise she had a certain power. 'Undo this for me.'

Susie hesitated then moved forward and unclipped the bra. Stephanie did nothing. 'Well take it off me then,' she ordered testily.

Susie obeyed, leaving Stephanie standing in the cabin in her dark grey suspender belt, sheer cream stockings and high heels.

Stephanie could see the man's eyes staring at her body. The altercation had not diminished his erection. She was enjoying herself. She was in charge. Somewhere behind all this, she knew, was Devlin, but for the moment she was in charge, flying at 35,000 feet and six hundred miles an hour, and she knew she could do and have anything she wanted.

'Hold his cock.' Susie obeyed at once, obviously having decided that Devlin's instructions in relation to Stephanie overrode any other considerations. Stephanie resumed her position, pushing backward on to the man. She felt Susie's hand on his cock and felt her guiding it into her still-wet cunt.

'Now my clitoris,' she said. The thrill of being able to order a woman to do something so intimate practically brought her off at once. She managed to restrain herself because she wanted to feel his spunk inside her and let that make her come.

Susie's touch on her clitoris was perfect. The man's cock felt even bigger now. She could feel it swell. She knew he was going to come and she knew her orgasm was there too. As she felt the first hot jets of spunk spray into her cunt her whole body shook with her climax making her scream with pleasure and grind her body further back on to the man to get him just that inch deeper so she could finish with it there, as deep as it would go.

Stephanie didn't want to move but when she felt his cock slip out of her she straightened up.

'Is there a bathroom?'

Susie nodded and, collecting Stephanie's clothes, led the way back into the main cabin. There, set in the forward bulkhead, was a complete bathroom with a powerful shower, bidet, toilet and every possible toiletry from shampoo to perfume, all recessed in custom-built mirrored cupboards.

'We'll be landing in fifteen minutes, madam,' Susie said, emphasising the *madam* as if to confirm Stephanie's authority. But Stephanie was not finished with her new-found power. She had had another idea.

'Wash me please.' She indicated her suspenders with a nod of her head and immediately Susie unclipped them and rolled the stockings off as Stephanie raised each leg in turn. Then Susie unclipped the suspender belt and ran the shower.

When the temperature was to her satisfaction Stephanie stepped into the warm water. The shower was strong and pummelled her body, making her feel fresh and clean again. Susie took the soap and washed her back, hesitating for a moment only when she came to the front, waiting, perhaps, for Stephanie's approval which was given with a nod of her head. For a moment Stephanie considered ordering Susie to perform a more personal service but at this stage she decided she did not want to over-indulge herself and settled for letting Susie wash and dry her, and help her back into her clothes. With this amount of luxury, over-indulgence was something she would have to be careful to avoid.

Back in the main cabin, fully dressed again, Stephanie felt refreshed.

'Who is that man?' she asked Susie.

'I don't know, madam.'

'Is he going to the lake?'

'Yes, madam.'

'What will happen to him there?'

'I don't know madam.'

Susie clearly knew more than she was prepared to say but Stephanie thought it was pointless to ask further questions. She ordered a small glass of champagne which she sipped as the plane banked and came into land. How much of what had happened on the flight had been planned by Devlin in advance she did not know and, she had to admit to herself, she did not care. The experience in itself was enough.

Chapter Three

As the plane taxied to a halt on what was obviously a private landing strip Stephanie could see a large black Mercedes waiting on the tarmac. The plane came to rest near the car, the pilot shut down the engines and Susie opened the exterior door and deployed the landing steps built into the fuselage of the plane.

'I hope you had a pleasant flight, madam,' Susie said mechanically without looking directly into Stephanie's eyes. Stephanie said nothing in reply, stepping out into the balmy heat of an Italian evening.

The uniformed chauffeur held the back door of the car open for her and Stephanie climbed in and watched as Susie handed the driver her case.

At the back of the plane a van had driven up and parked and Stephanie saw two men manhandling a large coffin-shaped crate off the plane. Susie went over to supervise. Obviously the other 'passenger' was not going to have quite as comfortable a ride to the castle.

It took only five minutes to drive to the lake. It was only as they arrived at a large wooden jetty that Stephanie realised there had been no passport control or customs at the airstrip where they had landed. Either they had entered illegally or Devlin was a very influential man in Italy. What looked like a brand-new motorboat, in highly polished wood and brass, waited at the jetty. Stephanie was guided on to the back transom and immediately the engines were fired and the boat glided away from the moorings. Then the engines were opened up and the boat surged forward cutting a huge swathe through the calm water and leaving a vast foaming white wake to mark its passage.

The sun was setting now. Whether this was part of Devlin's plan too Stephanie did not know, but the view from her seat was one of the most breathtaking she had ever seen. She could see the castle on an island in the middle of the lake and behind it the sun setting in a fire of gold and orange. A flock of birds, disturbed by the noise of the engines, took to flight, flying out towards the sun, black silhouettes against the light.

With the power of the engines it took only a few minutes to cover the two or three miles to the castle. Stephanie thought she saw a glint of binoculars as they approached, a servant perhaps, going to alert Devlin that the boat was on its way. And sure enough as they approached an ancient wooden jetty built at the bottom of a long stone staircase leading up into the castle, a staircase overhung by bougainvillaea and jasmine, she saw Devlin standing at the mooring, smiling energetically.

'Welcome, welcome!' he shouted as the boatman glided the boat into the rubber buffers and jumped ashore to moor the boat fore and aft.

He put out his hand to help her from the boat and she took it. The boat rocked slightly as she stepped on to the jetty. Seeing her hand in his again immediately sent a whole panoply of thrills racing through her. She remembered his huge fingers, each individually the size of a banana, the whole hand resembling an American baseball catcher's mit, but had thought perhaps her recollection had exaggerated their size. In fact, as she looked at them now, she realised her memory had added nothing to their dimensions. Her own hand was dwarfed by Devlin's: in his it looked like a small child's. The thought of what this hand, these fingers, would do to her later, and of what they had done in the past, made her feel a delicious shiver of anticipation.

'I'm so glad you could accept my invitation. I hope all the arrangements were satisfactory,' Devlin was saying.

'Everything was perfect, thank you.'

He was as ugly as she remembered too. His huge bulbous nose veined with blue blood vessels dominated his face, his pock-marked skin like the surface of some strange planet.

'I tried to think of everything.'

'It's nice to see you again.' And Stephanie meant it. She hadn't been sure what her reaction to seeing him would be after their brief but intense affair in London. But she suddenly experienced a strange rush of affection for this man: whether it was because of the way she was being treated, like some Oriental princess, or something more profound she did not know.

'I'll show you to your room and then we can eat. I think you'll enjoy the food. I've tried to make it special.'

'Why me?' It slipped out. She had been determined not to ask that question.

'The time we had together. You made a very great impression on me.'

'You haven't made any attempt to see me since.'

'I thought perhaps it was best to wait a while,' he said seriously, as though trying to make her believe it was something he had thought about at length. 'I can assure you I would like to see a great deal more of you in the future.'

Questions crowded into her mind again but she decided to ignore them all. The boatman had untied the motorboat from the jetty and started to nose out into the lake, no doubt going back to pick up the other visitor. Devlin indicated the stone staircase and she walked ahead of him – it was too narrow for more than single file – smelling the fragrance of the flowers and looking back over the lake, as the boat cut through the still water again and the sun finally set. Behind her Devlin followed, his eyes taking in her pinched ankles immaculately clad in the fully fashioned seamed stockings and soft Bally shoes he had chosen for her.

They passed a small courtyard planted with orange trees and through two massive carved wooden doors into the anteroom of the castle. A vast marble staircase dominated this area, leading to a long gallery on the first floor. Everywhere Stephanie looked there were objects of beauty: handwoven rugs on marbled floors, oil paintings, all modern and individually lit. The furniture – tables, chairs, little chests of drawers, a huge armoire, some antique, some modern – were works of art in themselves. Everything fitted perfectly against the grained stone walls of the castle.

Devlin led her up the marble staircase and along the gallery until they reached a thick, polished oak door at the end of a short corridor.

'This has the best view of the lake,' he said, leading her through the door.

The room was like a suite in the world's most sumptuous hotel: walls lined in pale cream silk, a deep pile navy-blue carpet, two cream sofas, and an elaborate modern four-poster bed made from ash and curtained in white voile. A white lace counterpane covered cream silk sheets. There were flowers everywhere, all colour coordinated with the room in shades of white and cream occasionally dotted with blue. Off to one side Devlin showed her the bathroom of white marble equipped with a huge bath and powerful shower and amply supplied with every size of fluffy white towels and matching bathrobes, all neatly folded on heated towel rails.

Devlin opened the french windows on to the terrace which ran the whole length of the bedroom. It was paved in terracotta tiles shaped into hexagons and furnished with loungers at one end and a table and chairs in white cast iron at the other. Here there were lemon trees in full fruit, individually planted in terracotta pots of the simplest design. On the castle wall honeysuckle and clematis, both dripping with heavily scented flowers, vied for position in the sun.

Stephanie walked over to the parapet and looked out across the lake. Devlin was right: the view was magnificent. Below her she could see the jetty and the little courtyard in front of the main doors. She could see the lush vegetation that seemed to grow from every crevice of the castle to form a cascade of flowers and, in the distance, as the last light faded, the land on the edge of the lake disappearing into the mists of twilight. The scent of the flowers in the still of the early evening air was almost overpowering.

Devlin stood by the bed as she came back into the bedroom from the terrace. He looked uneasy, as if trying to gauge whether he should approach her now or wait till after dinner. Stephanie kissed him lightly on his pock-marked cheek, having to stoop slightly as Devlin was not a tall man. Some men, in this situation, would have had no hesitation in claiming their prize.

'This is so beautiful. Everything.' She unbuttoned the dress and stepped out of it, standing in front of him in the cream silk underwear and stockings, wanting to make a deliberate statement with her immodesty. He took her hand purposefully and she had the feeling he wanted to say something, something important to him and necessary, but at that moment there was a sharp knock on the door.

'The luggage ...' he said, looking crestfallen. He took the case from his servant, opening the door only a crack so there was no possibility that the man could glimpse the vision that stood by the bed. The mood had been broken.

'Let me get changed,' Stephanie said.

'Of course.'

'We have all night.'

'You are a very beautiful woman. I thought so the moment I saw you that night in London.'

'Thank you. You make me feel very special.'

'Do I?'

'Of course you do, Devlin,' she smiled.

He walked over to the bedroom door.

'If you want to . . .' She was about to finish the sentence when she hesitated. She would actually have loved him to come over to her now, push her knickers aside and cram one of his massive fingers into her cunt so she could have that unique feeling once again.

'No, you're right. We have all night,' she said, trying to convince herself.

'So come down when you're ready.' He left her alone in the room.

Stephanie stripped off her underwear and showered again. She took the black lacy basque out of the case and clipped it on to her slim body. This was the surprise for Devlin she had bought yesterday, after trying almost everything in the lingerie shop. She knew she looked at her most sexy in a basque. It accentuated her small waist, firm tits and full hips and when she had clipped the sheer black stockings into place the thin black suspenders snaking out over her thighs made her long legs look even longer. At the back the tight black material above her waist emphasised her full round arse and, perhaps by contrast to the constriction above, made it look somehow more available. She picked up a pair of black high-cut knickers and was about to slide them over her ankles when she thought better of it.

Knickers were superfluous to requirements tonight. She slipped her feet into her highest heels and stood looking at herself in one of the full length mirrors with which the room was well furnished. She watched her hand in the mirror, like the hand of a stranger, as it stroked the thick bush of her pubic hair, teasing out her clitoris for a second, producing the faintest thrill.

As objectively as she could she assessed the reflection in the mirror. The tight black satin and lace basque hugged her body, the stockings shimmered, the band of flesh above them white in contrast and infinitely inviting. It was not possible for her to look more sexually aware, she thought. And her body was alive, sexually alive, in a way she had never experienced before. After what had happened on the plane, after having fucked a man she had never met and whose face she had not seen, it was not surprising. But it was more than that. She was removed from reality, here in this lush medieval paradise. There was nothing to do, nothing to think about, but her sexuality. She felt like an animal must feel. Everything else stripped away but her body and her feelings.

She turned from the mirror and slipped into the strapless black evening dress provided by Devlin. Her cleavage, well supported by the bra of the basque, pushed up and together, formed a long dark tunnel between her breasts. She had no need to shadow it with blusher. She turned to her make-up. In a few seconds she applied mascara, lipstick, eye shadow, making sure it was all heavier, bolder than she would normally have used. She wanted to look like a whore. An expensive whore, certainly, but a whore nevertheless. That idea excited her: she was going to enjoy playing her part tonight.

The dining room was lit with candles. A sheet of one-inch-thick glass supported on pedestals of polished steel provided a dining table quite big enough to seat twenty or more people. Two places had been laid at the end closest to the fireplace where a fire of apple logs produced its unique heady fragrance. Devlin stood by the fire, gazing into its depths, as Stephanie walked in. He was smartly dressed in a suit and tie but there was something about Devlin that made even the best tailored clothes look slightly scruffy.

'Enchanting, my dear. Simply enchanting,' he said. His voice was deep and rich, certainly his most attractive feature.

'This was your choice?' she said indicating the dress.

'Yes.'

'You have very good taste.'

A servant appeared and poured Stephanie a glass of champagne from a bottle sitting in a silver cooler on one of the many coffee tables. He wore a white linen jacket with gold-braided epaulettes. The tall crystal flute he handed her was edged with gold. Devlin picked his glass from the mantelshelf and clinked it against the side of hers.

'To our weekend.'

'To our weekend,' she repeated, looking straight into his eyes.

'The castle gets cold in the evening even in the summer. Such thick walls, the heat never gets through.'

'The fire is perfect.'

'We'll eat. You must be hungry after all your ... exertions.' He hesitated before using the word as though wanting to make sure he chose one with the right connotations. Stephanie wondered if he had received a report of her activities on the plane. She was sure Susie would be anxious to tell all.

Taking her hand Devlin guided her to the table, kissing her hand before they sat down. In front of her she recognised the distinctive pattern of Georg Jensen silverware, and the delicacy of the finest bone china. Almost instantly a waiter served wine and sparkling water. Devlin tasted the wine fastidiously but his eyes never left Stephanie, seemingly studying every detail anew, though often probing the dark shadow of cleavage resting above the black silk of the evening dress.

It was a remarkable meal. Delicate sea-bass, followed by baby lamb – a specialty of the region according to Devlin – and a simple salad. Wonderful tastes but not filling. They chatted amiably, enjoying each other's company again as they had done in London. Devlin's range of interests and knowledge was wide, his conversation witty and amusing.

'Would you mind if I skipped dessert?' Stephanie asked.

'Not at all, my dear. Coffee?'

'Espresso?'

'We are in Italy.'

She declined the offer to move to the sitting room for the coffee, preferring instead the intimacy of being eye to eye and elbow to elbow with Devlin at the table. The waiter brought cups of strong espresso coffee and a small silver platter of petits fours. Stephanie had the impression that Devlin was nervous. Despite all his money, all his obvious power and influence, he was still unsure of how to broach the subject of sex. Fortunately Stephanie had no such inhibitions. She was enjoying herself too much for that. This was a game she was delighted to play.

'I would like to take you to my bed now,' she said moving her leg against his under the table.

'I would like that very much.'

'I'll make sure you do.'

Devlin started to say something then stopped. He sipped his coffee instead, then tried again. 'When we met in London . . .'

'When we met or when we fucked?' Stephanie said, smiling broadly. She was in no mood for euphemisms.

'It was very special for me.'

'And for me. You are a very ... unusual man.'

'Exactly. That's exactly what I wanted to say. I'm an unusual man. I seem to need unusual experiences to ...'

'Turn you on?' she suggested.

'Yes.'

'Like the painting in your bedroom? The woman with the crimson cunt?' In London Devlin's erection seemed to have been dependent on a curious, though very beautiful, painting of a naked ménage à trois.

'Yes. And other things.'

'Sounds fascinating. Tell me more. What other things?'

'Things you might find ... unacceptable.'

'And if I did? Find them unacceptable I mean?' She was teasing him.

'We could just be friends, of course,' he said, looking disappointed.

She took his hand, once again startled by how small it made her own look, and stroked the thick hair that grew above his knuckles.

'I'm a big girl Devlin. You'd be surprised what I can find acceptable. You'd be surprised what I can enjoy.' And Stephanie meant what she said. She had come a long way since she had met Devlin three months ago. Martin had led her along a road that she had no idea even existed but it had thrilled her, it had opened her, it had given her a sense of herself that she'd never had before. She had no idea what Devlin wanted this time but she knew this whole situation thrilled and excited her in the same way that her experience with Martin had done. She was at a point where she could accept and enjoy almost anything; it was a point of no return.

Devlin touched her cheek with the back of his huge hand, a remarkably tender touch.

'Not only are you an extraordinarily beautiful woman, you are obviously exceptional in other ways.'

'It's probably something you sensed in me. You made the right choice.'

'So it seems. More coffee.'

Stephanie wanted to say that she didn't want any more coffee, that she wanted him to stuff those enormous fingers deep into her cunt, nestling hot and exposed and probably wet, after all this talk, under her dress. But instead she said nothing, got to her feet and walked into the hall and up the stairs to the bedroom. She did not look behind her but heard Devlin following in her wake.

As she reached the ninth or tenth step she stopped and bent down to her ankle, taking it in both hands. From there she used her palms to smooth the nylon of the stocking all the way up her long leg, as though there was a wrinkle in it that she could not bear to tolerate for one moment longer. She reached the clip of the suspender and adjusted it to hold the stocking more tightly, her skirt hoisted up and out of the way. Devlin, standing stock still at the bottom of the staircase, watched transfixed, his eyes rooted to the white thigh above the black welt of the stocking. As she let her skirt fall back into place Stephanie glanced down over her shoulder, pleased at the look of pure lust she had created in Devlin. That, after all, was the idea.

In the bedroom she unzipped the black silk dress and let it fall to the floor. She stepped out of it as Devlin walked into the room, closing the door behind him. She stood in front of him in the black basque, sheer shiny black stockings and high heels, her legs apart, her arms akimbo. Devlin sat in one of the armchairs opposite the bed.

'This was my idea,' she said indicating the basque.

'What can I say? You're exquisite.' He touched the fingertips of his massive hands together in front of his mouth, as if in an attitude of prayer. He had a strange look in his eyes, a mixture of greedy desire and an almost thoughtful appreciation of aesthetic beauty. The thick black pubic hair was too dense for him to see Stephanie's labia but that was where his eyes seemed to rest.

'Do you like my breasts?'

Stephanie reached down into the bra cup of the basque and extracted her left breast. She pulled it up to her mouth and was just able to tease the already erect nipple with the tip of her tongue. Then she flattened the bra cup under the breast so it was fully exposed. She followed the same procedure with the right breast. She had practised it at home last night. The flattened bra still gave support to the breasts, pushing them up and out. Stephanie caught a glimpse of herself in the mirror and could not suppress a shiver of secret pleasure at what she saw. She was ready.

'What do you want me to do then, Devlin?' she asked.

He did not answer for a moment. She had no idea what he planned, but the anticipation was driving her pulse rate up.

'Nothing,' he said.

Very slowly and deliberately Devlin got up out of his chair and walked over towards the bathroom. For the first time Stephanie noticed that, set in the silk panels that covered the walls, was a small door, almost like a cupboard door. Devlin had taken a key from his pocket and was unlocking it.

'Come over here.'

Stephanie obeyed.

'I'm going to dim the lights. Then I want you to open this door.'

He found the light switch and all the lights in the room dimmed to a shadowy gloom. Stephanie put her hand on the door. Her breathing was shallow, her mouth dry, a knot of expectation tied tight in the pit of her stomach. Though it was only seconds time seemed to stand still before Devlin spoke again.

'Open it.' Devlin's voice was commanding now, all reticence gone.

Stephanie pulled the handle of the door and it swung open. Her eyes were not yet adjusted to the dim light, so what happened next was a blur of shadows. Two men plunged through the open door. One immediately came behind Stephanie and clamped one hand over her mouth, so she couldn't scream, and the other under her arm and around her chest. The second hoisted her feet off the ground and together they carried her over to the four-poster bed and dumped her on it. Almost as a reflex she tried to sit up but one of the men had climbed on to the bed, grabbed her wrists and swung his body over hers to kneel above her, holding her hands to either side of her head. Her eyes adjusted to the light a little and she could see the man above her had dark hair and dark brown eyes with a well-muscled but hairless body. His only clothing was what looked like a black leather jockstrap cut so tight it covered only his penis. But the pouch was hard, as though the leather had been stretched over a metal form, and too small and tight to allow room for an erection. It was held in place by thin metal chains padlocked at the waist. The other man was dressed in the same way but his body was a mass of thick curly fair hair and he was altogether heavier and beginning to run to fat.

Stephanie felt a hand moving towards her cunt. She snapped her legs shut and tried to buck the kneeling man off her chest. Her action had little effect. A hand grabbed at her ankle pulling it towards the corner of the bed where, despite her attempts to kick herself free, the Hairy Man strapped it into a padded leather cuff and secured it to the bottom post of the bed. They had come prepared. He took the other ankle and pulled it to the opposite corner. Gradually her legs were being scissored open, her cunt exposed. She continued to struggle but not from fear; she could feel her excitement growing. The other leather cuff was secured, her legs locked open.

Stephanie strained her head to see Devlin. He had pulled up a chair to a few feet from the side of the bed and was leaning forward, watching intently. His eyes looked strange, as if in a sort of trance. His mouth was open and his lips were wet, just touching the tips of his fingers which he still held in an attitude of prayer.

Now the hand was back on her cunt and this time there was nothing she could do to stop it. Fingering her clitoris briefly, it plunged two fingers deep into her cunt. Stephanie moaned. It was no surprise to her that her cunt was already wet with her juices. The man kneeling above her bent to kiss her on the mouth. Stephanie responded at once wanting this contact, wanting to be part of the proceedings, wanting to use as well as be used. The man's tongue probed her mouth and she took it eagerly, sucking it as if it were a cock and then pushing it aside with hers so she could penetrate his mouth. He released her hands from his grip but she made no attempt to use them.

She felt the weight lift from her body as the man on top of her broke the kiss and moved to her side. His hands teased at her nipples, pinching the tight corrugated flesh. She closed her eyes to wallow in the sensations her body was experiencing. She was no longer sure whose mouth, hands, fingers or tongue was doing what to her; it just seemed they were all over her body, biting, nipping, pinching, caressing, plunging into mouth, cunt and arse.

She felt a tongue, hot and wet, tapping at her arse. She felt a finger sliding along her clitoris, another mouth biting her nipple hard, a tongue licking her face, even her eyelids, and then a finger pushing into her arse alongside the one already embedded in her cunt. They drove into her in unison. She was smothered in sex. There was so much sensation that her first orgasm seemed almost irrelevant. It had come as one of the men chewed on her clitoris, sucking it whole into his mouth and using his tongue to probe the hard knot of nerves. She tossed her head from side to side. She moaned. With her hands she tried to clutch at the men's genitals, desperate to feel a cock, but all she could feel was the unyielding leather of the pouches so tightly fitted that there was no way she could worm her fingers under the leather to achieve her objective. Somewhere in the back of her mind she knew, of course, that the only cock she was going to be allowed was Devlin's cock.

She had forgotten, for the moment, about Devlin. She opened her eyes and looked round to find him standing close to the bed looking down at the three of them. He was naked now but his penis was flaccid. Stephanie looked into his eyes. They seemed to be pleading with her, pleading for something he was not prepared to put into words. But she knew what it was.

'Stop it! Stop it!' She screamed catching the hair of one of the men's heads and yanking it back, pulling his mouth off her breast. Tears sprang to his eyes. 'Get off me, you animals. Get off!'

The sudden ferocity of her attack took them by surprise and Stephanie landed two or three hefty blows before they realised what was happening. Then the Hairy Man, the quicker of the two to adapt to the new situation, tried to catch one of her flailing arms. After two abortive attempts he got hold of her left wrist and held it with both his hands. Immediately Stephanie tried to prise his fingers away with her free hand but this gave the other man his chance and he grabbed her right wrist and pulled it away. They stretched her arms apart, at right angles to her body and flat on the bed so that she was spread-eagled. They knelt either side of the bed pulling her arms so tight she couldn't move, couldn't lever herself off the bed at all, couldn't resist.

'Let me go! Let me go!' she screamed, struggling still though her attempts to free herself were futile. She turned her head to look at Devlin. She did not smile – that would have destroyed the illusion – but Devlin's erection was massive now, just as she remembered it, a cock of gigantic proportions, veined, gnarled and ugly. She felt a rush of excitement centred on her cunt.

'You bastards. You bastards! I'll cut your balls off for this!' She struggled, her body beginning to sweat with the effort.

'Hold her,' Devlin commanded. The words clearly thrilled him. His cock shuddered.

'You're not putting that thing in me! I can't take it. Please don't. Please. I'll do anything. Let me go. Please let me go.'

Devlin came round to the foot of the bed and knelt between her outstretched legs. He put one of his massive fingers at the entrance to her cunt then, looking her straight in the eyes, he pushed it home. She tried to keep the pleasure out of her eyes but the feeling his finger produced was so intense she didn't know whether she succeeded. Her memory had not betrayed her; to have a hot finger of this size inside her was a feeling quite unlike any other. As he pushed it up into her she could not suppress a moan of absolute pleasure. After a moment she came, a sharp intense biting orgasm that racked through her pinioned body.

'You bastard. Get it out of me!' she shouted, recovering quickly. She fought the hands that held her, her actions contradicting her words as she writhed herself down on to Devlin's finger. It was making her come again. She couldn't control her body, her orgasms. 'You bastard, you bastard.'

It was all part of the game she knew. It was a wonderful game, a game that was thrilling her every bit as much as it was Devlin. She knew what he wanted and it seemed she wanted it too.

The two men tightened their grip on her wrists, perhaps at a sign from Devlin. She looked at them both, twisting her head from side to side, and saw their greedy eyes taking in every detail of her prostrated body, the black silk basque, its bra pushed down to reveal her breasts, the black stockings pulling at the suspenders, one of the stockings heavily laddered now, and her slim ankles tied into the leather cuffs, but kicking to be free. Stephanie knew their cocks, restrained under the tight pouches, must be aching for the space to spring to erection. And she knew they would not get it, certainly not with her.

'Hold her now,' Devlin said again.

His finger was out of her and he was moving his cock up to her labia. She could feel its heat radiating like a hot poker.

'No! No! No!' One final effort, she thought. 'No!' She screamed at the top of her voice. 'It's too big. Please, *please*!'

The sound of her voice turned her on as much as she hoped it did Devlin. His cock moved into her only an inch at first, but that was enough to swamp her with feeling. His cock was so wide her cunt was stretched in every direction. Then he pushed forward and she was suddenly filled with him, filled so full she could think of nothing but his cock. She felt another rush of juices flooding from her cunt. She felt him push again and go deeper. She looked down, straining her head off the bed, and could see his cock was still not fully home. She knew she couldn't take any more. Orgasms were ripping through her body one after another, one continuous orgasm now, as she could not tell where one ended and the next one began. Devlin was fucking her. Moving his cock in and out supporting himself on his arms so he could look down and see his penetration. Each inward stroke seemed to be stronger and go deeper. Then he lay on her and kissed her on the mouth, his tongue probing into her.

She wrested her mouth away from his and screamed. This was his game and she knew how to bring him off, wanting to make him spunk inside her, wanting to feel that spunk jet out of him deeper than any man's had ever spunked in her. She knew how to make him come.

'You dirty bastard. You filthy slimy bastard. Get that filthy thing out of me. I'll kill you!'

She felt his cock swell even more and knew he was coming. The extra width took her breath away but she managed to control herself. She felt his spunk spurt out of him, felt his cock spasming inside her and heard him gasp with pleasure in a sound wrenched from his heart. Suddenly she realised her hands were free. She wrapped her arms around his back and he kissed her lightly on the lips. Her ankles were freed too, and as he rolled on to his side she nestled up alongside him.

'You're a remarkable woman,' he said. Out of the corner of her eye she saw the two men crawling back through the little door in the wall, their black pouches still firmly in place. Her mind, not for the first time this weekend, filled with questions, but she pushed them aside, wanting only to enjoy the aftermath of her orgasm.

For the first time since she had come into the bedroom she was aware of the gentle lapping of water on the shore of the island and the scent of bougainvillaea from the terrace. It had been the most extraordinary day of her life, from the chauffeur-driven limousine to the private plane and now this. What tomorrow would bring she did not know, but she had the feeling it would be quite as exciting as today.

As she lay there on the silk sheets drifting off to sleep against Devlin's warm body, her mind replayed the scene that had just taken place. Stephanie knew that though she had been, for all intents and purposes, the helpless object in Devlin's rape fantasy, the fantasy that had brought him to erection and orgasm, she had not been in the least helpless. In fact, she had been the centre of his passion, she had created the fantasy for him, controlled and used it to bring him off when she had so desired. In a strange way it had given her a feeling of power over him and, she realised, it was a feeling she savoured. All the exquisite sexual feelings she had experienced that night in the game of rape had undoubtedly turned her on; but she knew also that the fact she had used that game to manipulate a man like Devlin, with all his wealth and power, to do what she wanted when she wanted it, was what had thrilled her most.

Chapter Four

Stephanie woke feeling relaxed and rested. She was alone in the bed. Whether Devlin had gone in the middle of the night or first thing in the morning she did not know; he had certainly not disturbed her sleep. She stretched out in the bed and immediately felt a stiffness in her cunt and nipples. Considering the exertions of the night it was no surprise. She stroked her pubis rather as one would stroke a cat and after a few minutes it felt better. Her nipples were a different matter: they were positively sore.

At dinner last night she remembered Devlin had said she should swim in the lake in the morning. Now she couldn't think of anything she would rather do so, slipping on the practical swimsuit Devlin had provided, and pulling on one of the fluffy white towelling robes from the bathroom, she took a towel and wandered down through the castle and the flower-draped stone steps to the jetty. Not a soul appeared to be about. Hanging the robe on one of the wooden posts she dived into the water. It was a wonderful sensation. The water was warm and silky and when she opened her eyes underwater she realised she was swimming among scores of fish. She turned on her back and floated, her

44

face picking up the heat of the morning sun. Then she flipped over on to her stomach and swam fast in an effortless front crawl, wanting to stretch and work her muscles.

After thirty minutes of this exercise she felt refreshed and extremely hungry. Pulling herself on to the jetty she was surprised to find one of the servants standing, her robe in his hands, waiting to help her into it.

'Mr Devlin asks if you will join him for breakfast,' the man said in English flavoured with an Italian accent.

He turned and walked up the stone steps and Stephanie followed, using the towel she had brought to dry her hair as she walked. On the other side of the small courtyard by the main doors was a small flight of steps up to a large open terrace, once again garlanded with flowers and terracotta pots, and tiled in what she imagined to be local ceramics. Here Devlin sat in front of a circular table laid for breakfast with white linen napery.

'Good morning, my dear. The swim was a good idea, was it not?' Devlin rose and kissed her on both cheeks.

'Wonderful. The water is so soft. It's like silk. And all the fish.'

'Yes. Surprisingly they seem not to regard man as any threat.'

A basket of croissants and brioches was set on the table with honey, jam, butter, a plate of sliced melon, and glasses of blood-red orange juice. A servant brought large cups of steaming espresso coffee. Stephanie ate with abandon as Devlin watched. Now, she thought, would be a good time for some of the questions that had crowded into her mind last night.

'Our chef makes the croissants. He tells me it is quite an art.'

'They're delicious.' And they were.

'I hope you didn't mind me leaving you this morning.

There were one or two calls I had to make.' He looked genuinely concerned that she might say yes, she minded a lot.

'You didn't wake me,' she said instead.

'Good.'

'There's something I wanted to ask you, Devlin,' she said, taking the bull by the horns.

'Anything.'

'Your private plane ...'

'Oh yes. I understand you had a good look round.'

'I'm not stupid enough to believe you weren't told exactly what happened.'

'I was.'

There was a pause as though that was all there was to be said on the subject. But Stephanie had no intention of leaving it there.

'Who was he?' she said getting to the point.

Devlin smiled broadly but did not reply.

'Is he here on the island now?'

'My dear, I wanted to give you the best possible weekend you could imagine. One of my staff thought that the plane could carry another passenger. It was not part of my plan. If you'd remained in the cabin, of course, you would have been none the wiser ...'

'But I didn't.'

'No.'

'Your stewardess used the expression "on punishment". What did that mean?'

'You don't miss much, do you?' Devlin sighed. 'Why don't you just forget it? Let's enjoy our weekend together.'

Stephanie looked Devlin in the eyes. 'I want to know,' she said firmly but quietly.

'It is a very delicate matter.'

'I can be discreet.'

'You may be shocked.'

She smiled broadly. 'I thought I'd convinced you last night that I am not easily shocked.'

'Well, you'd better see it all for yourself then. If that's what you want.'

'It's what I want,' she said emphatically.

'As soon as we've finished breakfast, then,' Devlin conceded. There was no arguing with the determination in Stephanie's voice.

Stephanie drank her coffee slowly. She was in no hurry. She had won her point. Devlin looked distinctly uneasy about revealing whatever secret the castle held but she knew he was committed now and would not go back on his word. The sun was getting hotter and it felt strong on her face. She pulled off the robe and let the sun dry her swimming costume as she saw Devlin's eyes moving over her body, no doubt remembering the glories of last night.

She chose a thin white suspender belt, matching bra and lacy French knickers with sheer white stockings. Over this she wore a silk dress in creamy white that buttoned down the front, and white shoes with heels not quite as high as those she had worn last night. She brushed out her long black hair and then pinned it up rather severely. As she had a long neck and good, firm chin, the absence of hair falling to her shoulders always somehow made her look taller and more in control.

She joined Devlin in the sitting room where, in one corner, he had a large desk and shelves and cabinets of papers and books.

'Ready,' she said smiling.

'I've never seen you with your hair up,' he commented.

'Well?'

'I like it.'

'A lot?'

'Yes.'

He got up from the desk and led her by the arm out into the marble lobby. Beside the main staircase Devlin pulled aside the corner of a large modern tapestry, draped over much of the wall, to reveal a small thick wooden door which he unlocked with a key from his key-chain. Behind the door Stephanie felt a rush of cool air and saw a flight of steep winding stone steps leading down into the cellars of the castle. She shivered slightly.

'Be careful,' Devlin warned.

He indicated a thick rope looped to the wall along the length of the stairs before leading the way down. She grasped the rope and started down after him, wishing she'd worn the flatter heels. The steps were narrow, the stone worn away by centuries of use. They led to a broad, vaulted brick chamber lined on all sides with racks of wine. Devlin made no comment. Stephanie knew little about wine except that this amount must represent a considerable investment in financial terms.

Devlin was standing at the far end of the long chamber now, in front of another strong-looking wooden door set into the stone wall.

'Are you sure you want to know?' he asked, though he knew what her answer would be.

'Yes,' she said immediately. 'Don't look so worried. I'm a big girl.' She patted him gently on the cheek.

Devlin rapped twice on the door. After a moment Stephanie heard a lock turn and the door swung open. A man stood in the doorway dressed for all the world like a medieval executioner: black tights, black tunic, black boots. All that was missing was a black hood. He was a big man with the physique of an all-in wrestler.

'This is Bruno. He's a mute, so I'm afraid he can't say hello.'

'He's clearly not a fashion victim.'

'Oh, I dress him like that for my amusement. Just a little joke.'

Bruno stood aside and Stephanie followed Devlin through the door.

'Bruno's father used to work here in the castle before I acquired it. And his father before that. Actually I don't think Bruno has ever been to the mainland.'

Again they were in a brick-vaulted chamber but this one had been divided into a long corridor with small cells running down both sides. All the cell doors were the same size, all contained circular peepholes that could be opened and closed and all were numbered. These may have been the castle's original dungeons but they had been renovated and remodelled in modern times.

Devlin opened the peephole to the cell marked with the number five.

'I believe you've already met this gentleman.'

Stephanie gazed through the door. Sitting on the floor in the little cell was the man in the mask. He was naked except for the same hard black leather pouch that the men had worn last night and a thin chain around his neck bearing a metal disc engraved with the name CLIVE. Around one of his ankles a steel cuff was attached to a chain that was in turn locked to a ring in the stone floor. Seeing the peephole open, Clive stared at the door as though expecting something to happen.

'The names are entirely fictitious,' Devlin explained. 'Now the others . . .'

They went to each cell in turn, opening the peepholes. Behind each Stephanie saw the same sight: a man or a woman, chained by one ankle, the men in the hard leather pouches, the women naked, all wearing a disc bearing their Christian name around their necks. Each looked up at the door as they saw the peephole open, some apprehensively, some apathetically. Two of the men Stephanie recognised immediately. They were the men Devlin had used last night, though they had not worn identity discs then.

Stephanie's astonishment was complete. Whatever she had imagined was happening at the castle since she'd seen the man in the mask, it was not this. For a moment she couldn't think which question to ask first. She looked at Devlin. He was clearly excited, his eyes sparkling and alert, at showing off his 'collection'.

'Do you want to know more?' he asked. He would have been disappointed if she had said no.

'Of course . . .'

'These . . .' he hesitated, trying to avoid using the word 'slaves', '. . . people were all employees of my various companies. They were caught with their hand in the till, so to speak. I offered them a simple choice. To come here to the castle and perform certain services or to be handed over to the police.'

'What services?'

'During the day, cleaning, gardening, domestic work . . .'

'And at night?'

Devlin smiled broadly. 'With a business the size of mine I have many friends, acquaintances, colleagues. I can sympathise with people who have special sexual needs, as I'm sure you understand. I have organised this castle to meet their needs. They, in turn, can be very helpful to me and to my business. Needless to say, because of the position of my . . .' This time he didn't hesitate. '. . . Slaves, I can guarantee their complete discretion. None of them would dare breathe a word of what goes on here.'

'How long do you keep them here?'

'I try to make the punishment fit the crime. Usually six months is the maximum. After that exhaustion sets in.'

'So the man in the mask? He's one of your slaves?'

'Yes and no. He is a slave now certainly but that is his

choice. That is his fantasy, his need if you like. The mask is to protect his identity. He's quite a well-known figure. Even my slaves might be tempted to go to the tabloids . . .'

'How intriguing.'

'Apparently your treatment on the plane gave him considerable . . . eh . . . pleasure. I think you can say he now owes me a very large favour.' Devlin was grinning broadly. He turned to Bruno, who stood impassively, his arms crossed over his muscular chest. Devlin ordered him to bring champagne which he did at once, much to Stephanie's relief. She definitely needed a drink after all this. Sipping at the Dom Perignon from the tall crystal flute, she could not help but feel a sense of excitement. It was like being in the middle of a fascinating sexual dream except, quite clearly, this was not a dream.

It was not long since all this would have come as a shock to Stephanie. But that was before she had embarked on a voyage of sexual discovery. She had become fascinated with sex, bought books on every aspect of sexual behaviour and found that a great deal of what she read had turned her on. That had led her into the affair with Martin who had given her experience of what she had read. It had turned her on more than she would have believed possible; it had created a whole new dimension for her. Now she stood in the middle of a whole world of sex created by Devlin, more, she suspected, at least at first, for his own gratification than for so-called 'business' reasons. Of course, in the event it was no doubt extremely beneficial to his interests, having powerful, influential men not only in his debt for sexual favours they would find it difficult to obtain elsewhere, but trusting him enough to let him into their secrets. No wonder Devlin had all this. She took another large swig of the champagne.

'Perhaps we should have a practical demonstration?' She

could hear the excitement in his voice, hoping she would say yes but too timid to insist.

'I thought you'd never ask.' Stephanie wanted to make him feel at ease, wanted him to know she had taken this whole experience in her stride. His diffidence towards her was unnecessary. She was committed.

Devlin walked up to cell number eight. Bruno took a key from his belt and at a sign from his master unlocked the door. Stephanie followed Devlin into the cell, handing Bruno her empty champagne flute as she did so.

'You see we cater for all tastes.' Devlin said.

The woman in the cell was fat, but in a strange way the fat was not disproportionate to her body. It was the sort of body that Rodin painted, large fleshy tits with big nipples and brown areola, a round plump arse with dimpled cheeks and a round fleshy navel. The flesh was not lined or sagging. It was firm with a bloom on it like a fresh peach. Like all the female slaves the woman was completely naked except for the disc which announced her name as Dolly. Immediately the cell door opened the woman assumed a kneeling position, her head bowed forward. In this position her large tits rested on top of her thighs.

'The rule of the house is that all slaves must obey without question. You are a thief, aren't you, Dolly?'

'Yes, master.' The woman did not raise her head to answer the question.

'She is remarkably attractive, don't you think? Considering her size.'

That was exactly what Stephanie thought. In fact she could not take her eyes off the woman's body. In her mind's eye she could see herself lapping at those huge tits or burying her head in between her ample thighs to get at her clitoris. She realised she was squirming slightly, rubbing her thighs together almost without realising she was doing it.

'What shall we do with her?' Devlin was stroking the woman's hair now, very much as one would stroke a favourite pet. It was cut short and streaked with blonde highlights. 'What shall we do with you, Dolly?'

'Can I make a suggestion?' Stephanie said boldly.

'Of course . . .'

'I'd like to see her with Bruno.'

'Oh no.' Devlin chuckled. 'I'm afraid Bruno had an unfortunate accident some years ago which, shall we say, left him disinterested in these proceedings. That's why he's so useful to me down here. We could always have him whip her, of course.'

'No, master, please no.' There was real fear in the woman's voice.

'Why don't you suck me then?' Devlin said.

The woman looked up for the first time. She had blue-grey eyes and looked pleased to have avoided a whipping as she unzipped the front of Devlin's slacks. His penis was flaccid. She disentangled it from the front of his boxer shorts and slipped it into her mouth.

'Some are more cooperative than others. Dolly is exceptionally docile. Bruno has only had to deal with her twice. Hasn't he?' The woman nodded, trying not to let his cock slip from her mouth in the process. His cock was still flaccid. Stephanie watched as the woman worked away on it, sucking, licking, doing everything she knew to try to make him hard. But none of it worked. Devlin was looking at Stephanie now, that same look he had used last night. For some reason he was not prepared to ask her for what he wanted but that did not diminish his need.

Stephanie unbuttoned the silk dress and stepped out of it. She pulled the stockings taut, one after the other, before slipping her fingers under the loose crotch of the french knickers and along her labia. As she had imagined it would be, her cunt was already moist. Hooking her thumbs into the waist of the knickers she drew them down to her ankles and stepped out of them. She picked them up from the floor. The crotch was damp. She took it over to Devlin and held it against his face.

'This is what you do to me.'

'Really?' He inhaled the fragrance of her body as he felt the warm silk on his face. Stephanie looked down to see his cock pulse and swell in the woman's mouth.

'Devlin,' she whispered, making sure he could feel her hot breath in his ear, 'I want her. I want you to watch. I want you to see me with her.'

His penis grew again. Dolly worked it in and out of her mouth. Stephanie could see it was wet with her saliva. The ample flesh of Dolly's body quivered as she moved.

In the corner of the cell was a plain wooden bed with a thin mattress. Stephanie got up and lay on the bed, bending her knees and opening her legs, the white stockings emphasising her nakedness above the thighs. She stroked her clitoris with her finger. She knew what she was going to say next and she knew it would arouse her in the saying.

'Come and sit on my face.' She wanked her clitoris and slipped two fingers into her cunt, feeling a flush of sexual excitement. Dolly stood up and came over to the bed. Devlin watched as she positioned herself, knees on either side of Stephanie's body, and then lowered her round fleshy arse on to Stephanie's face. Suddenly Stephanie was surrounded by flesh, soft, warm, jelly-like flesh. She reached up with her hands to claw at the mammoth tits that rested on her naval as Dolly lent forward, uninvited but not unwelcome, to gobble at Stephanie's cunt. Stephanie's fingers found the nipples and pinched at them viciously as her tongue found, buried deep in the layers of flesh, the long clitoris of Dolly's cunt.

Stephanie felt she was drowning in flesh. On top of her were acres of flesh pressing into her body. It was an exquisite sensual experience, especially as Dolly's tongue and mouth were expertly manipulating her cunt, the tongue flicking at her clitoris while her arms wrapped themselves around Stephanie thighs so the fingers of both her hands could play with her cunt too. Stephanie felt four fingers, two from each hand, pushing into her. Instead of going deep, however, they tried to widen Stephanie's cunt, to pull it apart, like opening a drawstring bag. This was an entirely new sensation for Stephanie. Perhaps because of Devlin's size she was particularly sensitive in this area but she found herself coming almost at once, and coming with a special intensity.

She tried to return the compliment, but with Dolly bent forward it was hard to get to her cunt. Then it occurred to her that there was no need. She was there to give Stephanie pleasure. Her own was immaterial. There was no necessity for Stephanie to reciprocate. The thought struck her with the same force as a physical attack. Devlin had given her the power over this woman and it was the thought of this power that, she knew, made her come in Dolly's mouth, just as much as the urgings of fingers and tongues.

She pushed Dolly off her and gulped in air. Then she looked around to see Devlin standing by the bed wanking at his huge erection. She remembered her amazement when she had seen him do it before in London. A normal cock would have been engulfed by his huge hand. But Devlin's cock protruded from his clenched fist as he wanked it up and down.

'I want to see her suck you off, Devlin.' Stephanie almost did not recognise the sound of her own voice. It was harsh and wilful, but it was a sound that perfectly reflected her mood. It was the sound of authority. She was in charge here now.

Dolly crawled over to Devlin's cock and sunk it into her mouth.

'I want it deeper,' Stephanie insisted, knowing full well there was no way anyone could take the whole of Devlin's cock into her mouth or cunt. But Dolly tried and it slipped in another inch. 'Give her your spunk, Devlin. I want to see it.' Stephanie barked out the command. 'Do it, Devlin.'

Stephanie was standing in her high heels, suspender belt and stockings and bra, her legs apart. Devlin feasted his eyes on her. He watched as Stephanie took Dolly's head in her hands to control her rhythm as she plunged down on Devlin's cock. He looked her straight in the eyes, their faces only inches apart, and saw a determination there, a determination to make him come. He felt his balls tense. He felt the silky wet mouth sucking on his cock and Stephanie's eyes boring into him, commanding him, and then he came, shooting spunk into Dolly's mouth and watching as a smile of satisfaction and triumph spread over Stephanie's face. She saw what he had done, what she had made him do.

Stephanie had the impulse to lean forward and kiss Devlin on the mouth but she resisted it.

She realised that Bruno was still standing by the cell door, impassively watching all that had happened. With a gesture from Devlin he unlocked Dolly's ankle chain and led her away, no doubt to be showered. Devlin sat on the wooden bed.

'Only you could have done that to me,' he said quietly.

'I know,' she replied with absolute confidence.

Chapter Five

*U*pstairs it felt hot. Devlin had gone off to take a telephone call somewhere in the depths of the castle, leaving Stephanie on the terrace where they had breakfasted. She sat on one of the loungers sipping what had become the accustomed champagne, and debated whether to go and change into her bikini to take advantage of the sun. The Italian sun had almost reached its zenith but a cooling breeze from the lake made the temperature tolerable. For the time being Stephanie was content to relax, enjoy the magnificent panorama laid out in front of her and wait for Devlin to return.

The Devlin who finally came back on to the terrace was a very different man from the one who, happy, buoyant and relaxed, had left Stephanie some half an hour before. This Devlin suddenly looked old and tired, the worries of the world settled on to his shoulders. He tramped across the terrace, his whole demeanour suggesting his anxiety.

'What on earth's the matter?' Stephanie asked, genuinely concerned.

'I'm afraid something has come up. Business. I've got to go to the mainland right away. I'm sorry . . .'

'Anything I can do?'

'No, no . . .' Though his eyes were looking at her she could see his mind was somewhere else entirely.

'When will you be back?'

'Probably after lunch. I'm sorry. It's unavoidable.'

'Don't worry about me. I'll sunbathe. It's so hot.'

'If you want lunch, they'll bring you anything you want.'

'Thank you.'

'And make yourself at home. There are no locked doors for you.' He looked reluctant to leave her.

'Devlin, go. I'll be fine. There are no more secrets, are there?'

'No. You've seen it all.' Devlin smiled weakly but the worried frown soon returned. 'If you want Bruno, dial 5 on the phone.'

'And I don't expect him to say hello, right?'

This time he did not manage a smile. She saw one of the servants waiting with a large briefcase as Devlin shuffled off, clearly totally absorbed in whatever problem had suddenly cast a shadow across his world. Surely, Stephanie thought, with such obvious wealth, it could be nothing too disastrous.

She watched from the terrace as Devlin climbed aboard the motorboat and turned round to see if she was still on the terrace. He waved distractedly when he saw her and she waved back as the boat pulled away from the jetty, then sped over the almost still waters of the lake, leaving a foaming white wake.

One of the servants poured her a glass of champagne. She had never drunk so much champagne in her life and it felt good. It was, she decided, her favourite drink. The maximum of intoxication with the minimum of alcohol, though she would have been intoxicated enough without any. The secrets of the castle were revealed. Most of the questions answered. She remembered that she had not asked Devlin about Venetia and made a mental note to do so when he returned.

Taking her champagne she sat on one of the loungers in the full sun, feeling the sun on her face. In the distance she could still hear the faint roar of the motorboat's engines carrying Devlin to the mainland. What the problem was she could not imagine but, to be honest with herself, she was glad of the chance to be on her own and let her mind digest what was happening to her. She thought of going up to her room and lying in the sun on her terrace, as she wasn't yet ready for lunch, but for the moment she had no inclination to move.

As she lay with her eyes closed against the sunlight she let her mind wander back to the cellar and its occupants. Remembering the feelings she had felt as she lay on her back drowning in Dolly's flesh, she could not help an involuntary shiver of pleasure. She got up and walked into the house, telling the servants she'd have lunch in an hour. But as she walked to the staircase and mounted the first few steps she stopped, reversed her direction and headed instead for the small wooden door hidden behind the tapestry drape. The cellar was pulling her back. She had felt the same with the masked man on the plane, a force like a magnet, invisible, but impossible to resist. She wanted more, though more of what specifically she had no idea. More of something.

The cellar door had been left unlocked. Was that Devlin anticipating her needs? She grasped the rope at the side of the stone steps and walked down into the dimly lit cellars. She wondered, as she rapped twice on the door to the cells, whether Bruno would let her in on her own, but when the door swung open he seemed almost to be expecting her and stood aside immediately to let her in.

She said nothing to him and walked up and down the

corridor looking into the cells more carefully this time. One of the women, a tall blonde beauty with long hair and long slender legs, particularly caught her eye. Stephanie noticed thin red marks on the top of her thighs and imagined she had been whipped. Of all the slaves this woman looked the most discontented. But Stephanie did not feel in the mood for a challenge or another lesbian experience. As she contemplated the tall blonde she realised that what she actually wanted was cock. She wanted to be fucked. That was what she had missed this morning. She wanted a hot live cock deep inside her cunt. As she thought about it the need grew and became urgent.

There was no way to compare the cocks of the male slaves, as they all wore the hard leather pouches. She would have to go on general appearance and hope for the best. She could, of course, have Bruno strip the pouches off but that would have taken too long and she was in a hurry. In the second cell was a stocky, hairless and reasonably attractive man in his late thirties. He had a good firm body and short dark hair with an alert and open face.

'Number two,' she ordered. Bruno opened the cell without question.

The man assumed the position she had seen Dolly adopt with Devlin, kneeling with his head down. Stephanie went over to him and stroked his hair gently, very much as Devlin had with Dolly. He did not look up, and she took his chin in her hand and forced his head up so he had to look into her eyes. His name-tag read: *Adam*. She could not tell what was in his mind, whether it was fear or anticipation or disinterest. Whatever it was she suddenly laughed out loud. She continued to laugh as she took her dress off for the second time this morning.

Bruno still stood in the doorway of the cell. Stephanie considered sending him away but decided against it. There was no point. In fact, the short riding crop tucked into the belt of his tunic had given her an idea, an idea that excited her more than she would have imagined possible after this morning's activities. She removed her bra and saw that her nipples were already hard. It was as though she had saved them earlier, not wanting Dolly to finger them, so that they would be fresh and alive now. She stripped off the stockings wanting to be completely naked this time, and then stood in front of the kneeling man.

'Pull my knickers down,' she ordered.

He reached up and found the waistband, pulling the french knickers down to her ankles and she stepped out of them. He bowed his head again as though he were not allowed to look at her naked body.

'Put your head up again, Adam,' Stephanie said, allowing annoyance to enter her voice. He obeyed at once. She stepped forward slightly and pushed her pubis into his forehead, feeling its hard bone against her fleshy mound. His mouth, in this position, was between her thighs and she could feel his hot breath on her cunt. She pressed her pubis into him rhythmically, as though she were fucking his forehead.

'You're very lucky, Adam. You're going to fuck me. A straightforward fuck,' she lied.

She got on to the bed, which was identical to the one she had lain on in the other cell. For the second time that morning she lay on her back, bent her knees and opened her legs. For the second time her cunt felt incredibly hot and wet. She knew that a lot of her excitement was in this power that Devlin had given her, this ability to command whatever she desired. She had always been turned on by words, had always wanted her lovers to talk to her and her to them, always loved being told that she was going to be fucked or sucked or buggered and now she realised that her voice – hard and strange – issuing unequivocal orders was turning her on as much as anything else.

She noticed Bruno's eyes had not left her for a moment.

'Fuck me then,' she said impatiently.

Adam stood up, looking pathetically down at the hard leather pouch chained over his genitals. Stephanie had forgotten about that.

'Get it off him, Bruno. Quickly.'

Taking a key Bruno roughly spun the man round and removed the little padlock from the thin chains that held the pouch in place. Suddenly freed from the constriction that had lasted for god knows how long, Adam's cock sprang into a rigid erection.

'Come on,' Stephanie said, wanting no further delays, the level of her arousal increasing every moment.

The man did not need further bidding. There was to be no foreplay. He fell on Stephanie and in one movement his cock was buried inside her. It was not the size of Devlin's of course, but it was good to feel the base of a cock grinding up against her clitoris again, a feeling no woman would ever achieve with Devlin. He was thrusting madly, violently as though he hadn't had sex for weeks. Stephanie took his hair in both her hands and held it tight. She moved her mouth to his ear and whispered in the most menacing tone she could muster: 'Stop now.'

He obeyed immediately, though she could feel his penis pulsing involuntarily inside her.

'Bruno, use your whip.' This was her idea. Bruno took the whip from his belt and in one fluid, practised motion, striped it across the man's buttocks. His penis bucked into Stephanie. Calling for the whip, hearing herself saying those words, had brought her to the edge of orgasm.

'Again,' she ordered, holding herself back, wanting to stay on the edge and in control and not be plunged into the abyss of a climax. Again the whip came down and Adam's penis drove into her propelled forward like a pile-driver. She ordered the whip again. His penis bucked.

She clung to his hair and screamed with pleasure as Bruno's strokes fell on Adam's naked arse and she lost control, allowing herself her orgasm and feeling it course through her body unleashed at last. How many strokes landed before he came she did not know or care. But she knew she was ready for his spunk and felt it jet out into her seconds after the whip drove his cock into her again. She had never felt spunk so hot. It felt like liquid fire. She heard herself scream with pleasure as his spunk spurred her orgasm to a new intensity.

It was minutes before she realised she was still grasping his hair. She let go and had to stop herself apologising as she could see it had brought tears to his eyes. How silly to think of saying sorry, she scolded herself. Why should she care? It was an attitude she intended to get used to.

During the aftermath of her orgasm Bruno must have left the cell, as he now offered her a white towelling robe. She extracted herself from the man and put in on. With a movement of his hand Bruno indicated that she should follow him, which she did, not bothering to look back into the cell as she left.

At the far end of the corridor, opposite the entrance, was another stout wooden door. This opened on to what looked like a conventional suite of rooms, decorated with the same lavish style as the rest of the castle, except, of course, for the absence of windows. Light was provided by a series of tastefully arranged spotlights, big lamps and by the lights illuminating every picture. The rooms had a strange feeling, a feeling of secrecy and decadence.

Obviously anticipating Stephanie's needs, Bruno showed her to a large marbled bathroom. She showered and towelled herself dry on one of the large stock of fresh white bath towels neatly folded on the heated towel rails. As in her own room, the bathroom cabinet was stocked with expensive toiletries and Stephanie selected a moisturiser and annointed her body with it. The cool liquid felt good on her skin.

Pulling on the towelling robe again, Stephanie walked back into the corridor of the suite. Bruno had gone. She wandered through the other rooms. There were two large bedrooms, each with king-sized beds, one with a mirror on the ceiling above the bed. Both rooms had televisions and video recorders but there were no tapes that she could see. Presumably this was where Devlin's 'friends' brought the slaves for various sexual athletics, perhaps preferring not to be seen with them above ground. Or perhaps their appetites could not wait to be satisfied quickly once they had seen the opportunities laid before them.

The remaining room in the suite was less conventional. It had the same stone walls and floor as the cellar outside and the lights were harsher and brighter, though they could be dimmed. But it was what the room contained that fascinated Stephanie. Months before, before her affair with Martin, before sex meant anything more to her than simple fucking, she had come across the first of many books, a book on the more outré sexual dimensions. It had fascinated and enthralled her. She had bought other books and read them all with an equal relish. It was as though she had stumbled into a secret world, a world that existed behind closed doors, a world she had never suspected or dreamt of. But she had known that it was a world she would, sooner or later, want to explore. And that had led to her affair with Martin. Martin had shown her around that secret world. It had scared her, she had to admit it, but it had also thrilled her. It had given her sexual pleasure she would never have dreamt possible.

Now, as she stood in this room, the impact of reading that first book came flooding back to her. The room contained everything she had read about. There was every conceivable piece of sexual equipment, handcuffs, leather straps, ball gags, chains hanging from the ceiling and from the walls, punishment frames, a stock and a wooden rack. There was every type of whip, crop and paddle, and every size of dildo. A strong pulley, threaded with nylon rope attached to padded cuffs, hung from the ceiling. Three large wardrobes stood against the further wall. Stephanie opened each in turn to find them full of leather and rubber clothing, high-heeled shoes and a selection of wigs. There were drawers of bras, panties, suspender belts, corsets and stockings, all neatly arranged by size.

It was all here. Bondage, rubber, transvestite, sadomasochism. It was all here in this room. Every fantasy could be catered for. In this room it would be possible to bind a man or a woman, dressed in rubber, leather, or whatever, in any position one cared to imagine. And do to them whatever one cared to do. There would be no escape. The illustrations in the books she had bought had always been line drawings, not photographs; drawings of men and women tied in extremis. Because they were drawings they had not appeared real; in this room the bondage would be only too real. The thought sent a chill through Stephanie. Then she thought of what Devlin had said about the slaves. They were all thieves. And in this room they would get their punishment. Of that she was certain. The frisson of fear she had felt as she contemplated these devices turned to a little knot of excitement. She would not like to be on the receiving end of any of this equipment. Or would she?

In a sense Martin had tortured her. Not physical pain, admittedly, but he had put her into bondage. She walked over to the pulley tied off on a cleat screwed into the stone wall. She unwound the white nylon rope from the cleat and let it loose. Immediately from the centre of the room the other end, attached to the leather cuffs, descended. She went over to where they hung at head height and inspected them. Fitting one on to her wrist she felt the thick padding inside the leather, very much like the cuffs that had held her last night. She tightened the strap on one wrist and stood with her hands high above her head, as high as she could reach. She closed her eyes and felt the strain in her shoulders. Could she imagine herself standing there bound and naked, not able to bring her hands down to relieve the pressure, waiting helplessly to be whipped or handled or fucked in any way her tormentor wished?

She bought her hands down and unbuckled the cuff. Her hands were trembling slightly. The stretching had loosened the towelling belt and as she pulled the belt free to retie it, the robe fell open and she glimpsed her naked body. Both her nipples were puckered and rigid, as hard as she had ever seen them.

Chapter Six

The sun was high in the sky and heat radiated in a shimmering haze from any surface not protected by shade. Stephanie had changed into the bikini that Devlin had provided, a costume definitely not capable of withstanding exposure to water. Cut high on the hip, it showed off Stephanie's long legs and tight curved bottom while the spangled tiny bra did little to conceal her breasts. The wrap, designed to be worn with it, was no more than a thin veil of chiffon. Coming down to the main terrace Stephanie had ordered a light lunch of lobster and salad and had decided against more champagne. She sipped ice-cold mineral water instead and had been tempted by the offer of ice cream after the salad. The melon ice cream the waiter had brought was unbelievably delicious, but she avoided the temptation to gorge herself on it. As she had thought on the plane, the main problem this weekend was to know where to draw the line. From where she sat the view over the lake was breath-taking, framed by the cascading flowers, the sun reflected off the almost still water. The heat of the sun made her body feel calm and relaxed.

The secrets of the castle were hers now. It was extraordinary that Devlin seemed to trust her implicitly with all this. He had been true to his word: There had been no locked doors, either physically or metaphorically – she had been able to go and do whatever she had wanted. Had Devlin not been so obviously distracted by his long telephone call Stephanie would have thought him quite capable of deliberately leaving her alone to see what her reaction would be, to see what she would do or perhaps to draw her deeper into the web.

The waiter brought her a steaming cup of espresso coffee. She left it to cool and walked over to the parapet of the terrace and looked down to the lake below. She could not see the stone steps leading down to the jetty as they were completely covered in the twining bougainvillaea and jasmine but she could see the jetty itself and the water of the lake softly lapping at its wooden supports. She could hear the noise of the water from here too. Whatever Devlin imagined she would feel standing here on his terrace, the beauty of the castle and the island all around her, her mind able to dip into the memories of the morning in the cellars and the pleasures of last night, Stephanie had to admit her reaction was rather curious: she felt strangely at home.

After a second cup of coffee she decided to go upstairs to her terrace and lie out in the sun. Devlin would be back soon she thought, so this was her chance for a little sunbathing. Back in the bedroom she noticed the underwear she had discarded in the cell this morning had been washed and neatly folded in a precise pile on one of the chest of drawers.

Outside she positioned one of the loungers to catch the full sun and lay, feeling the heat boring down on her body. She closed her eyes. Quite unexpectedly, in her mind's eye, she saw herself strapped into the leather cuffs in the punishment room of the cellar suite, hoisted by the pulley on to tiptoe naked and helpless. She opened her eyes again to free herself of the image then, in a matter of seconds, she was asleep. Dreams swarmed into her head, dreams that were so realistic as to be more memories than dreams. She saw Devlin kneeling between her legs, his huge cock erect, his banana finger already inside her. And then her sleep deepened and there were no dreams at all.

Only a few minutes later she awoke, feeling unusually refreshed. But she was hot, the delicate bikini streaked with her sweat. She walked into the bedroom to find some suntan lotion as she could feel her skin was already taking colour. In the bathroom cabinet, as she had come to expect in the castle, there was an expensive oil which she massaged into her face. Looking in the bathroom mirror she could see that even after such a brief exposure her face and arms were browning. She rubbed the thick white cream into her cheeks and forehead, looking at herself intently as she did so. Her eyes stared back at her, looking strangely knowing after the last eighteen hours. Her brown eyes were bright, the whites very white. Trying to be objective, she had to say she thought she looked very good. Sex obviously suited her. At least this sort of sex.

She went back into the bedroom and examined herself in the full-length bedroom mirror. The cut of the expensive bikini, despite the sweat, complemented her body perfectly. She had no idea what it cost but it was certainly more than *she'd* paid for an entire outfit. She felt good in it. She felt good in all the clothes that Devlin had given her. She loved the feeling of these beautiful materials made with the minutest attention to detail. All the clothes he had given her in the suitcase felt as if they had been made for her. They felt comfortable and elegant, and she knew they suited her. She felt at home in them. She had to say she loved the life here at the castle too. But then, who wouldn't? London, her job seemed to be in another world. Effectively, of course, it was another world, and one she had no desire to think about until it was absolutely necessary. And that time was not now.

The scent of bougainvillaea drifted in from the terrace on a light breeze. All she had to think about now was Devlin. And herself. He would be back soon so in the meantime she could enjoy the sun. Why she was lying in a bikini on what must be the most private terrace in Italy, she thought suddenly, she could not imagine. But if she was going to lie naked then she would need her skin oiled against the burning sun. She smiled to herself as she walked over to the phone on the bedside table. She had to dial five, she remembered Devlin telling her. Her smile broadened as she heard the phone ring twice before it was answered.

'Bruno, bring one of the men to my room right away.' She heard him hang up by way of reply.

The pleasure she took in issuing these orders was out of all proportion to the orders themselves. It was the sensation of being in command, a pleasure she had never experienced before, that she enjoyed. It was a pleasure Devlin had given her, created for her. There was no question in her mind that being able to command, in the way she had this morning in Devlin's cellar, had affected her deeply. She could hear her voice – that strange hard voice she had never heard herself use before – and remember what she said, what commands she issued. It was a part of the sexual experience, an integral part she knew, that had done more than given her an endless stream of orgasms. It had, in some way, defined her sexuality. Of course, Devlin was responsible. She had allowed Devlin to use and abuse her, she had enjoyed the game of 'rape'. But that was only the other side of the coin, the flipside. In a strange way, tied and held down on the bed last night, helpless as she was physically, she had still been in control. She had given Devlin his pleasure. The game he had begun she had hijacked. She had started wanting to please Devlin, certainly, but something else had taken over: all that eventually mattered was that she had pleased herself. Ironically, she thought with delight, the more she pleased herself, the more she seemed to gratify Devlin.

She wondered if Devlin would get a report of her activities while he'd been away. No doubt the servants had tracked her movements but she did not know how he could get information from Bruno; he did not look as though writing was one of his talents. Not that she wanted secrecy. She wanted Devlin to know precisely what she had done. She could always tell him herself.

The knock on the door pulled her out of this reverie.

'Come in.' She heard her hard cold voice again.

Bruno entered, followed by a man dressed in a one-piece nylon work suit elasticated at cuff and waist and with a long zip running from neck to crotch. Bruno immediately indicated, in effective sign language, that the garment should be removed. Under it the man was naked save for the hard black leather pouch chained tightly around his genitals and, of course, the name disc on the chain around his neck. The disc read: *Paul*.

'Out on the terrace, please.' Stephanie made a mental note not to use the word 'please' again in these circumstances.

She stepped out into the sun and the two men followed. She pulled the thin shoulder straps of the bikini bra down over her breasts. She watched Paul's eyes staring at her tits, the nipples already hardening under his gaze.

'What's your real name?'

'I'm not allowed to say, madam.' His voice was reedy and uncertain.

'You're allowed to tell me.'

Bruno shook his head vigorously and put a finger to his lips, presumably to indicate the need for silence. But Stephanie was not prepared to obey Bruno, just as she had not listened to Susie on the plane. Stripped to the waist, her firm tits hardly bouncing on her chest, she walked over to him.

'I don't want to have to tell Mr Devlin that you have not cooperated with me, do I, Bruno? He wouldn't like that, would he? What would he do if he didn't like it, Bruno? What would he do if I told him you had refused me?'

For half a second Bruno stared into Stephanie's eyes with a look bordering on contempt. But the thought of Devlin's displeasure was too powerful a totem to ignore, as it had been for Susie. Bruno dropped his eyes to the floor and studied his feet.

'So your name is . . .' Stephanie returned to the slave picking up the metal name tag in her hand.

'Norman, madam.'

'See,' she said looking at Bruno. 'That's wasn't too difficult, was it, Norman?'

'No, madam.'

'I have much more difficult things for you to do in a minute. How long have you been here, Norman?'

Bruno's head came up again as if to intervene but Stephanie was already looking at him defiantly and he quickly thought better of it.

'Four weeks, madam.'

'Oh, so you'll be quite experienced then.'

'If you say so, madam.'

'So polite. I like that.'

Stephanie pulled the bottom of the bikini down over her thighs and, bending over, pulled it off her ankles. As she bent down, her arse nudged against Norman's thigh. His eyes had followed every movement and as she bent over he could see clearly the long slit of her sex, and the lips of her cunt covered in curly black pubic hair.

The terrace was equipped with a double-sized lounger, a lounger of the usual design and length but of double width which could accommodate two people lying side by side. 'There's sun-tan oil in the bathroom, Norman,' said Stephanie, lying down. 'Bring it here. You're going to rub it in for me.'

Norman immediately disappeared inside. Stephanie stretched out, her legs open, her arms above her head. Almost at once she could feel the sun on her sex. It was a strange feeling. In England she had never sunbathed in the nude. She looked over to Bruno who still studied her feet, apparently showing no interest in her. He looked hot, his black costume more suited to the cool of the cellar than the heat of the sun.

Norman returned with the oil.

'You can start on my back,' Stephanie told him, rolling on to her stomach. Norman knelt by the side of the lounger, squeezing the thick cream on to her shoulder blades and then starting to massage it all over her back with both hands. He had strong hands and a firm touch and Stephanie closed her eyes to enjoy the sensation of the cold cream being worked into her already warm skin. Once he had finished her back he squirted more cream on the top of her thighs and started to work on the back of her legs. Stephanie opened her legs again as he massaged her buttocks, knowing he was seeing every detail of her labia and puckered arse.

'Right down there, Norman.' This would be torment for him, she knew. His fingers spread over her arse and then down till she could feel them edging against her cunt. He started to move his hands away, down her thighs and calves.

'No, back where you were,' she teased. His penis must be straining hopelessly against the pouch now, unable to come to full erection, or find any release. His fingers kneaded the oil into the bottom of her arse again; they could not help brushing the lips of her cunt.

'All right, that's enough.'

With relief she could almost feel, his hands moved back down her legs to her knees and calves. She had considered getting him to massage her cunt properly but decided she wanted to relax: she was not going to go short of sex in the next few hours, that was certain.

She turned on to her back and looked straight at Norman. Her breasts were quivering slightly from the movement and she could see his eyes looking at them hungrily.

'Do you think I have a good body, Norman?'

'Yes, madam.'

'I let one of the slaves fuck me this morning, Norman.'

'Did you, madam?'

She could hear the edge of excitement creeping into his voice, reflecting a slim hope that she might just be planning the same fate for him.

'Get on with it then. Do my front.'

He squirted cream on to her navel and worked it all round her chest without actually touching her breasts. His hands creamed down to the triangle of pubic hair without touching that either. Then he worked on the front of her thighs and down to her calves and feet. Stephanie closed her eyes again, letting herself go to the delicious feeling the massage and the warmth of the sun were producing.

Since her remark about fucking the slave, Norman's touch on her flesh had changed. It was softer, more sensitive. He was no longer trying to keep himself detached, to view her as an inanimate object in order to keep his desire in check. Now it felt like foreplay.

'Take his pouch off, Bruno,' she ordered, opening her eyes to watch Norman's reaction. The slim hope was growing bigger, she knew. But Bruno was shaking his head vigorously. His eyes said this was the last straw and definitely not allowed. In the cellars he had not hesitated to remove Adam's pouch, so clearly there was some problem about doing it above ground. If it was a house rule it was an extremely silly one, Stephanie thought.

'I'm only going to ask you to do it once more, Bruno.'

He shook his head again.

'How do you think Mr Devlin is going to feel when he knows that his favoured guest, whom he has brought all the way from London, has been assaulted by one of his servants?'

Bruno shook his head from side to side in extreme agitation.

'Yes, Bruno. I've heard that even men who've had their cocks cut off get randy. But trying to assault me! Trying to get your hands up me! Not very nice, is it? I can't imagine what Mr Devlin will say. Let's put it this way, I don't think you're going to be working at the castle much longer, do you?'

The defiance in Bruno's eyes changed to fear. He came over to where Norman was still kneeling and taking a small key from the many on his keyring, he unlocked the padlock that held the pouch in place and pulled it away. Norman's penis, creased and reddened by the constriction, immediately sprung to full erection.

'You've forgotten to do my breasts, Norman. You don't want my breasts to get sunburned, do you?' As she said it she saw his erection swell again. She could see what he was thinking. Why else would she have had his pouch removed? She could feel his excitement as he squeezed the cream on to the palm of his hand and applied it to her breasts. He wasn't sure yet, though. He daren't allow massage to become caress as he felt the supple firm flesh and the tight rigid nipples under his hands. He could not prevent his erection nudging into her side as he stretched across her body to reach the furthest side.

Stephanie moved on to her side and looked down at his

penis. It was already weeping a tear of fluid and had left a little wet trail where it had rubbed along her side. She smiled to herself. If she were to take him in her hand now it would only be a matter of seconds before he came. She put her hand down under his cock and found his balls. She weighed them in her hand as if trying to estimate how much they held. She squeezed them not at all gently and Norman moaned. Then she let them go and laughed.

'Bring me some mineral water, Norman.'

Norman got up immediately and went into the bedroom hoping, no doubt, this was just a temporary delay. Stephanie watched his erection bobbing along in front of him as he walked. Bruno did not move. He stood as usual his arms crossed over his chest, his forehead wreathed in sweat, a look bordering on hatred smouldering in his eyes.

The water was ice cold and Stephanie sipped it before putting the glass, already wet with condensation, against Norman's penis.

'It must be very hot, Norman.'

'Yes, madam.'

'Do I make you hot, Norman?'

'Yes, madam.'

'Why is that, Norman?'

'You are very attractive, madam.'

'Would you like to fuck me, Norman?'

He hesitated, perhaps fearing that if he said yes it would provoke punishment.

'I asked you a question, Norman.'

'Yes, madam, I would.'

'A little more oil between my shoulder blades,' she ordered, turning on her stomach and putting the water down on the terracotta tiles. He knelt again and resumed the massage.

'That's enough,' she said. He stopped.

Stephanie lay still. Norman waited, his erection throbbing inches from her oiled flesh and the object that would give him release. He did not move. She knew that the temptation to throw himself on her, to bury his cock deep into that hairy open cunt was almost unbearable.

Laying on her stomach, her face turned away from the slave, Stephanie could not help but smile. Her body felt pampered, smothered in the rich oil and basking in the sun. She could feel Norman's tension and was enjoying it immensely. Occasionally over the next half an hour she moved around on the lounger and watched his greedy eyes search out every detail of her cunt and thighs and breasts. Not for a moment did his erection flag. If she cared to look she could see the engorged veins. He was uncircumcised and his foreskin still covered most of his glans. How he would love to reach down and pull the foreskin back, or better still, have her do it. Well, that was never going to happen and his disappointment was going to be complete.

The game was over. Her mood changed. She wanted some time alone before Devlin came back.

'Take him back, Bruno,' she said.

Norman said nothing but his eyes pleaded with her. He would get no relief in the cellars. This woman, with the hard cold voice, was not going to give him any comfort. He got to his feet. Bruno handed him the worksuit which he clambered into while Bruno picked up the leather pouch. They left. Stephanie noticed they used the little door that the men had used last night. It must be some sort of passage directly to the cellars.

Stephanie relaxed. Experimentally she ran a finger between the lips of her cunt. She was not surprised to find a wetness there. The knot of her clitoris felt hard too. But, without too much difficulty, she restrained herself from harder contact. Masturbation on this island would be like drinking water while sitting in a vat of wine. And in any event she thought she could hear the faintest hum of engines on the lake in the far distance. Devlin was on his way back.

She walked over to the parapet. Sure enough, in the distance, a dark speck was heading for the island. It did not take long before the speck became the definite shape of a boat cutting across the placid water leaving a white trail behind it. She watched, fascinated, as the boat got closer. She watched the wake of the boat, churned up by the propellers, gradually die away until the calm water re-established itself as though never disturbed. It was like watching the condensation trails of jets high in the sky as they gradually faded away.

She pulled on the diaphanous wrap. Though it was obviously intended to be worn with the bikini underneath, Stephanie had no intention of putting the costume on again. She slipped into a pair of high-heeled sandals and walked down through the castle to the jetty to await the boat's arrival. As the boat got closer she could see Devlin was sitting aft with another man. They were talking intently. She had expected Devlin to be alone. She pulled the transparent wrap around herself more tightly and thought of running upstairs to change, but then dismissed the idea as pointless and even faintly ridiculous. After what she had experienced already on the island modesty seemed distinctly out of place. It was a decision she would regret.

The speedboat glided gently into the jetty, the boatman expertly using the throttles to bring it smoothly alongside the rubber tyres hanging down into the water from the mooring. He cut the engines and jumped ashore to moor the boat forward and aft by brightly polished chrome cleats set in the varnished wood. Devlin stood up. He was smiling broadly, obviously delighted that Stephanie had come to greet him, his air of anxiety dissipated, she felt, but by no means vanished. As the boatman helped him ashore he turned to introduce the other man in the boat who had not taken his eyes off Stephanie, as far as she could tell, from the moment she had come into view.

'My dear, I'd like you to meet my associate Giancarlo Gianni.'

Gianni stepped from the boat on to the jetty. Stephanie offered her hand which he took in both of his and raised to his lips. As he pressed it to his mouth, she felt his fingers stroking her palm, almost as if trying to find a clitoris there. At the same time she felt his wet tongue dart out from between his lips to touch her hand too. She shook her hand free and did nothing to disguise her distaste. She would have rather been kissed by a three-toed sloth.

'Devlin has told me so much about you,' Gianni said, apparently oblivious to her displeasure.

'Has he?' She gave Devlin a sideways glance.

'But you are more than he has said.' Gianni was a stereotype Italian: olive skin, dark brown eyes, thick black hair, not tall but slim. He was probably the same age as Devlin but looked younger. He was impeccably dressed from his Gucci loafers to his Rolex watch and silk Valentino tie. His voice was low and his fractured English heavy with his Italian accent. 'More lovelier.'

'Lovely,' Devlin corrected. 'Shall we go in?'

'My apologies, lady. I have not to practise my English lately.'

'Don't apologise,' Stephanie replied with little sincerity.

The two men waited for her to go up the narrow stone steps first. Walking ahead of them in the thin wrap she might as well have been nude. She could feel their eyes feasting on her long legs, her round firm arse and the long slit between her legs. It was not a feeling she disliked. She heard Gianni say something to Devlin in Italian. From the tone of his voice she was sure the remark concerned her body.

On the main terrace the sun was not so fiercely hot. One side of the terrace was completely shaded by a giant hibiscus and the shade was welcome after the heat. Devlin ordered tea from one of the seemingly never-ending array of white-linen-coated servants and they sat at a table in the shade. Gianni sat opposite Stephanie. His eyes had not left her for a moment, dancing over her body, never quite sure where to rest or which part of her was most exciting. He looked, she thought, like a schoolboy in a sweet-shop, not sure of which of the goodies he should ogle over next. If she had to guess she would have said his gaze most often rested on the dark triangle of her pubis, thinly veiled by the wrap. His eyes were there now, staring intently as if trying to develop x-ray vision and see her naked cunt. He made no attempt to hide what he was doing, to look surreptitiously. Had he not been an obviously wealthy and sophisticated man she could well imagine him drooling from the corner of his mouth as he continued to stare.

As Stephanie might have expected, the tea arrived in a silver service, with delicate German china cups and saucers. Devlin dismissed the servant and poured the tea himself. Only Stephanie took milk. Both men used lemon. Despite his huge hands Devlin seemed capable of remarkable dexterity, passing the small cups to his guests with no spillage, cups that in his hands looked like the tiniest doll's house crockery.

Gianni watched as Stephanie sipped her tea.

'The English way?' he asked.

'Sorry?' She had no idea what he was talking about.

'With the milk. That is the English way?'

'Yes. But we have lemon too.'

'Gianni is an Anglophile . . .'

'Obviously.'

'I have an English car, Aston Martin. An English tailor, Huntsman. English sunglasses, Dunhill. English shoes,

Lockes. And I have many, many English women.' He laughed, dropping his gaze from her face to her breasts, wanting her to know that was where he was looking, wanting to get a reaction. He was disappointed.

'Aren't you the lucky one,' she said coolly.

'They, I would rather say, are the lucky ones.' He smiled broadly, pleased at his own remark.

'Really. Well, that's a matter of opinion.' Stephanie was developing a rapid dislike for this man. From the moment he stepped ashore her instinctive reaction was distaste, which was hardening into a very definite dislike. She had never liked arrogance in men. Gianni clearly thought his charm was quite irresistible and that any woman should be grateful to be graced by his presence.

'I'm English-craz*ee*,' he continued. Stephanie tried to look bored.

'Even his meat is flown in from England,' Devlin volunteered.

Stephanie laughed startling both men. She had no intention of being a piece of 'meat' for Gianni, if that was what Devlin had in mind. If he had come to the castle to experience the delights of the cellars, to have Devlin organise whatever sexual scenario he had in mind, in exchange for a quid pro quo to relieve the problem that had come up this morning, that was up to Devlin. But she had no intention of joining in. Not with Gianni.

'I think I'll go and change, Devlin.'

'But you look so elegant like this,' Gianni said at once.

'Have another cup of tea first.' Devlin took her cup. 'Gianni is right. You look wonderful.'

Gianni reached forward in his chair and put his hand on hers. She pulled her hand away. He put his hand on her knee. She looked down on it as if it were some fat slug.

'Do you mind?'

'Your flesh is so soft.'

81

'I prefer not to be pawed.'

He took his hand away reluctantly.

Stephanie gave Devlin the dirtiest look she could muster. Gianni was beginning to annoy her now, and Devlin was not going to escape her wrath. Now that she understood Gianni's penchant for the English it was dawning on her why Devlin had brought this particular man over to the island this particular afternoon. It was no coincidence. No doubt if Stephanie cooperated, and she had, after all, cooperated with everything else he had suggested so far, Gianni would be in his debt. The way Devlin was deferring to Gianni with an obsequiousness she would not have thought he possessed seemed to confirm her theory.

But she was not one of Devlin's slaves and had no intention of behaving like one. Devlin handed her another cup of tea. Quite deliberately she let the saucer slip through her fingers and it crashed down on to the unforgiving ceramic tiles where it smashed into a hundred pieces.

'I didn't want another cup,' she said in her frostiest tone, being sure not to apologise for the breakage. 'I'm going to change.'

She got to her feet. Both men did the same.

'I look forward to seeing you in a moment,' Gianni said, smiling broadly. Clearly his skin was extremely thick.

Stephanie walked into the castle. Obviously more sensitive than his guest, Devlin caught up with her at the foot of the stairs.

'Is anything wrong?' Devlin asked solicitously.

'Who is that awful man?'

'You don't like him?'

'I thought I'd made that pretty obvious.'

Devlin looked genuinely disappointed, a look Stephanie had not seen before. For a moment his years fell away and he looked like a little boy who'd just been told his favourite dog had died.

'He's a very important man to me at the moment. Very important.'

'I gathered that by the way you've been fawning over him.'

'I was hoping ...'

'That I'd provide some meat ...'

'That you might like each other. I can see he's crazy about you.'

'Cra*zee*,' she mimicked.

Devlin still looked pathetic. She had clearly been right about his intentions.

'There's at least two English girls downstairs, aren't there?' she said, trying to be helpful.

'Yes.'

'Devlin, you know I like you. But don't ask me this. Not with him. You can't say I haven't been cooperative so far.'

'Of course not. Forget it.'

But he didn't make it sound very convincing. Stephanie turned on her heels and ran upstairs. When she reached the landing she looked down and saw that Gianni had come in and was talking animatedly to Devlin. It did not take a genius to guess at the subject of the conversation.

Chapter Seven

*B*ack in her bedroom Stephanie fumed. The peace of this idyll had been rudely shattered by a boorishness of which she would not have believed Devlin capable. Up to now he had been charm itself, attending to her every wish. She had been only too happy to play his sexual games in return. But this was different. She was not a whore. If he had mistaken her compliance in his outlandish sexual games to mean that she was prepared to do anything in exchange for extravagant presents and lavish hospitality, he was sadly mistaken.

She tore off the wrap, regretting that she ever wore it, and went into the bathroom to run a bath. She only just heard the timid knock on the bedroom door over the noise of the water. She knew at once it was Devlin. Without bothering to put on a robe she flung the door open and stood in front of him naked, arms akimbo.

'What do you want?' she asked angrily.

'To explain,' he said.

'Explain then.' She went back into the bathroom and adjusted the flow of water. Devlin followed. He sat on the toilet seat.

'I know what you think.'

'What do I think?'

'That this was some sort of plan. I got you here this weekend for Gianni, because he's so keen on English women.'

'You're right. That's exactly what I think.'

'Stephanie,' he said quietly. 'It's not true.'

'I'm English-craz*ee*,' she said mimicking the accent again.

'I know, I know. I need him, Stephanie. I need him badly. I've got to get him to sign a contract this afternoon. That's why he's here. No other reason. If he doesn't sign ...' He let his expression of gloom finish the sentence for him.

'And you were going to help matters along by introducing him to the cellars?'

'No. No. It was strictly business. I need that contract signed. Now it's academic.'

'Why?'

'Because of you. He doesn't want to talk business. He just wants to talk about you. I don't blame him, I have to say. You looked stunning this afternoon. But I didn't plan it. Believe me, it's the last thing I wanted to happen. I wanted to get the damn contract signed and get him away again. So we could go back to our weekend.'

'Lust at first sight.'

'Exactly! I had no idea this was going to happen.' The look of anxious desperation had returned to his face. He looked like a man facing a firing squad. Stephanie felt sorry for him. And she was beginning to believe what he said.

'You'll work it out,' she said gently.

'I'll try. Please, let's try not to allow it to spoil what we had.'

'Deal,' she said kissing him on the cheek.

'I need that contract signed. Everything depends upon it.' He paused. He was looking at her but his mind was elsewhere. 'Everything.'

Stephanie felt he was genuine. 'It's just I don't go to bed

with men I don't like, Devlin. I never have. And I don't like him.'

She could not help a wry smile to herself. She hadn't even known the man who had fucked her this morning in the cellars, nor the masked man on the plane, so perhaps Devlin was justified in thinking her sudden acquisition of principles was rather odd. But, strictly speaking, since she had not known the men, she could hardly dislike them. With this syllogism she squared her moral tone. She knew Gianni, and definitely disliked him.

Stephanie's anger was assuaged. She turned off the water in the bath and tested the temperature of the water with her hand. Then she went and sat on Devlin's knee and stroked the contours of his face with the back of her hand. As her breast was closer to his mouth than her face, he bent slightly and kissed her nipple, then the top of her breast. He kissed her tentatively as though she might object. Stephanie hugged his face to her bosom. Her feeling of affection for him had returned; for the first time she sensed something in him she had not felt before. He seemed suddenly vulnerable as though the world were about to collapse around his shoulders, where he had carried it for years. Obviously his desire to please Gianni was every bit as serious as he had suggested.

Stephanie stroked the thick wiry hair on his head. She wondered if she could distract him from his veil of tears.

'What's Gianni doing now?'

'Sulking.'

'Seriously?'

'He's in the office. He's got some calls to make, if he can stop thinking about you for five minutes.'

'How long will it take?'

'An hour, maybe.'

'Does he need you?'

'No.'

'Good. So let's take a bath together. Then you can relax for awhile. You'll feel better.'

'That would be nice,' Devlin responded with no real enthusiasm.

He watched in the long mirror that ran the length of the bath as Stephanie undid the buttons of his shirt and stripped it off his shoulders. Still sitting on his lap she kissed each of his nipples in turn flicking at them with her tongue. Then she took his face between both her hands and kissed him on the mouth, pushing her tongue between his lips until it met his. As she kissed him she kept her eyes open. There was something sexually electric about this man: she could already feel a hard node of excitement tightening in the pit of her stomach. Perhaps it was his extraordinary ugliness, the pitted face and bulbous nose, or a chemical response, an overendowment of pheromones to match his overlarge genitals: whatever it was, the impact was startling.

'You're so sexy,' she told him honestly.

'Am I?' he said shyly as though a surprise to him.

She dropped to her knees and pulled off his shoes and socks. 'Stand up.'

He did as he was told and she unbuttoned and unzipped his trousers. They fell to the floor. She tugged his boxer shorts down to his ankles too and he stepped out of them. His penis was flaccid, as Stephanie had come to expect. With Devlin an erection had to be provoked by something other than nakedness: this afternoon, distracted as he was, this was probably doubly true.

'Sit in the bath. I'll wash your back.' Again Devlin obeyed meekly. Stephanie soaped his back lavishly, leaning over the bath, her breasts occasionally prodding his shoulder as she worked. She washed the soap off with a big sponge.

'Nice?'

'Very.' He meant it.

'Now the front.'

She repeated the procedure with his chest. Here the thick wiry hair meant she had to use more soap to get up a thick lather.

She climbed into the tub sitting in front of him, her legs spread out to either side. Conveniently the taps were sited in the middle on one side so they both could slide down the bath and rest their heads. She closed her eyes and squeezed her legs together slightly, feeling Devlin's hips between her calves.

'I went back to the cellars this morning after you'd gone,' she told him without opening her eyes. 'You knew I would, didn't you?'

'I thought you might.'

'Don't you want to know what I did?'

'Yes.'

'I got one of the slaves to fuck me. I don't think he'd been allowed sex for some time.'

'He was very ... ardent?'

'Very.'

Stephanie slipped her foot under Devlin's thigh until she could feel his balls resting on her toes.

'Do the same,' she said.

She felt his foot slide under her until his toes were brushing her pubic hair.

'Put your toe in,' she prompted.

Devlin pushed forward with no result.

'It's too dry.'

'Try again.'

She felt his big toe push against her labia, searching for an opening. She felt it nudge her clitoris and then work its way lower. She tried to wriggle herself down on to the toe but it was as though her cunt had been sealed over by the water.

'Won't work.'

'Push harder.'

'It'll hurt.'

Stephanie did not reply. She lay back in the water. The toe pressed forward again. It was still not in the right place. Devlin moved down further.

'There,' she said and he pushed hard, forcing his toe past the dryness of the labia into the heat and wetness of her cunt. Devlin pushed his toe deeper, enjoying the feeling. 'You must have some very imaginative guests, judging from all the equipment you have in cellars.'

'I told you we cater for all tastes.'

Stephanie moaned feeling his toe pushing forward again. The water had washed away her juices, reducing their lubricating effect and making real movement, in and out, difficult. Only the top of his toe, sealed away from the water, was really wet.

'Do you watch? What do they do? Have the slaves strung up and whipped? What do you like to watch, Devlin? What's your favourite? Tied down on the floor while you wank over them?' She squirmed down on his toe, enjoying the strangeness of the sensation. She was surprised at how it filled her cunt, but then perhaps his toes matched the proportions of his fingers.

'I've never been toe-fucked before.' She opened her eyes and looked at Devlin. His erection had risen like Excalibur from the bathwater.

'Can I fuck you properly?' he said.

By way of answer she climbed out of the bath, feeling his toe pop out of her cunt like the cork from a bottle of champagne. She bent over the side of the bath, opening her legs and thrusting her arse into the air, water running from her body on to the marble floor.

'Like this?' She looked into the mirror in front of her, staring into her own eyes but seeing nothing.

Devlin was out of the bath more quickly than she'd have

believed possible and she felt his cock now nuzzling her arse. It did not take long before it found the way opened by his toe. Her cunt was still dry. He pushed the tip of his cock forward but her cunt was unyielding.

'I want it, Devlin. Push harder,' Stephanie said. She didn't want foreplay. She wanted his cock to produce her wetness.

He pushed again.

'Do it for me,' she whispered.

He slipped his hand down to her clitoris but she pushed it away. She pushed back on to his cock. Suddenly she felt the first hint of her juices and his cock slid home a fraction. She pushed back again and this time she felt her wetness explode over the tip of his cock, like a sudden rush of water from a tap. His cock rammed home riding the back of this wave. The pleasure as she was stretched in every direction shot through her body once again. She couldn't believe she'd ever get used to it.

He reached forward and took her pendulant breasts in his massive hands. She looked down between her legs, as she had the first time Devlin had fucked her, to marvel at how much of him still remained outside her body. She supported herself against the bath with one hand and reached down with the other to grasp his balls. She managed to get both of them cupped in her hand.

'I can take more,' she lied.

'No.' But he pushed up into her anyway. In effect the movement took him no further forward, as Stephanie's cunt was already stretched to its limit but it was enough to bring Stephanie to the brink of a sudden, sharp, almost painful climax. Two more inward strokes and she was coming unable to suppress a scream as his penis hammered up against the bottom of her womb. Devlin mistook the cry for pain and withdrew a little.

'No. More. I can take it,' she hissed.

She squeezed his balls in her hand as if trying to pump his spunk out of them. She rotated her wet arse on his wet navel so his prick explored new areas of her cunt. She felt his prick pulsing inside her and knew he was coming. She squeezed his balls again, pulling them down away from his body.

'Do it. Give it to me. I want it,' she cried. And then she felt his prick swell to jet his spunk deep into her cunt as she heard him moan with the most tremendous relief. She looked up into the mirror and smiled at herself. It was over quickly but that was what she had wanted. She felt a real sense of achievement in getting Devlin to come with such comparative ease. She knew what to do now and knew it would work.

Devlin picked up two of the large bath towels and walked through into the bedroom sitting on the bottom of the bed.

'Come in here and I'll dry you off,' he said. The bathroom floor was running with water from both their bodies.

Stephanie came out, wrapping a towel around her hair turban style. She stood in front of Devlin who rubbed her quite hard with the towel, concentrating on drying her skin, ignoring the sexual potential rather as a father would a young daughter.

'Turn around,' he said in a parental tone. He finished the job, drying her back and legs and buttocks.

'There,' he pronounced. 'Finished.'

'Like being a little girl again,' and like a little girl she kissed him on the forehead. She felt like a daughter, he a father.

'About tonight ...' The spell was broken. What Stephanie had started was over. The worried frown had returned to Devlin's face, reflecting his concerns.

'Is Gianni staying for dinner, then?' Stephanie made his name sound like a dirty word.

'That's what I was going to say. Just help me . . .'

'I thought we'd settled that.'

'That's not what I meant. Just go downstairs and choose one of the English girls. Dress her up for dinner. There's wardrobes full of clothes in the next room. Get her to look really good. Get her to play along. He's got to believe she's really mad about him. It'll take the pressure off you.' He paused. 'I have to let him stay to dinner. Believe me, I wish I didn't.'

'I believe you,' she said and meant it.

Stephanie thought for a moment. She looked at Devlin. Whether it was deliberate or not the little schoolboy look had returned to his face and he looked like a twelve-year-old begging to be given extra pocket money to buy the model car he just had to have to complete his collection. What woman could resist? Not her.

'OK. I'll make her look so good he won't want any dessert.'

'Exactly,' Devlin beamed. The little boy was going to get his extra pocket money – the trouble was it might not be enough. 'Then we can have the rest of the night together.'

He hoped that was not a lie.

After Devlin had gone Stephanie went back into the bathroom and quickly washed her hair. As she dried it, watching herself in the mirror as she pointed the dryer, her mind wandered back to Devlin. It amazed her that she had been able to take so much of Devlin's cock, not only take it but enjoy it. She was pleased too that she had been able to provoke an erection in him without an elaborate charade. One day, it was possible that she would reach into those trousers and find a ready-made erection. She did not know how near that day was.

She examined the contents of the bathroom cabinets,

looking for the moisturiser and finding an Aladdin's cave of expensive toiletries. She was sure many of these items were not the sort of thing that a man would think to buy for a woman but everything she could possibly need was provided. Devlin had obviously employed a woman for this task. Suddenly Stephanie thought of Venetia again. She had been meaning to ask Devlin about her this morning, but, not surprisingly, it had slipped her mind. Where was she? Stephanie had certainly expected her to be here at the castle. She would ask Devlin over dinner, she decided.

She massaged moisturiser into her skin, lavishing it on her thighs and breasts and navel. She checked her toenails and fingernails to make sure the polish had survived the rigours of the day. She checked to see that the creases had fallen out of the blue evening dress she intended to wear for dinner. She laid out the blue silk teddy she had worn for Venetia in London, the night she had brought the invitation, and the suspender belt to match. This was definitely the night for sheer black stockings, in spite of the fact that the dress had a split skirt which would fall open to reveal expanses of thigh and therefore the black welt of the stocking top and above it the creamy white band of naked flesh. Let Gianni get an eyeful for all she cared. She was not going to let him spoil her plans. She had practised at home what she was going to wear, what went with what, and she had no intention of changing her mind in order to curb Gianni's ardour.

Devlin's idea of getting one of the girls from the cellars might work after all, though Stephanie doubted it. She knew which of the girls to use: the tall sullen blonde, her arse marked with the whip, whom she had seen on her lone visit that morning. Assuming from her appearance and colouring that she was English, she should easily be able to distract Gianni. She remembered her long legs, thick thatch of blonde pubic hair and her narrow waist that somehow accentuated her trim, up-turned breasts. She also had a look of disdain and since Gianni had apparently been so instantly turned on by her own disinterest perhaps that was what he would like best about the girl.

There was another one of Devlin's timid knocks at the door. Stephanie didn't bother to reach for a robe.

'Come in.'

'Charming, quite charming,' Gianni said as he walked into the room, only too happy to see Stephanie's naked body without the intervening veil of chiffon.

'Get out of here.' Stephanie picked up the towel Devlin had left by the bed and wrapped it around herself.

'You just invited me in.'

'I thought it was Devlin.'

'Devlin just left.'

'How do you know?'

'I was watching . . . and waiting.'

'You're supposed to be on the phone.'

'I can't think of business. You destruct me.'

'Distract.'

'Yes. I can only think of you.'

'I'm trying to get dressed.'

'Do not let me stop it. These things look delighted.'

'Delight*ful*,' she corrected again.

He was fingering the silk teddy, rubbing the material between thumb and forefinger, somehow making it look like an obscene gesture.

'You would look very . . . delightful', he said the word deliberately, 'in these.'

'Then perhaps you will excuse me.'

'You have the expression "Get off with the wrong foot"?'

'Yes.' She couldn't be bothered to correct him a third time.

'That is what we did, yes?'

'No.'

'No. Not the right expression?'

'Look, Gianni, I'm sure a lot of women think you're just great. But I'm not one of them. That's all there is to it. Simple.'

'Yes. See, I'm right. We get off with the wrong foot. I want you to like me very much. I like you very much.'

'Wanting isn't getting.'

'Pardon me?'

'You don't always get what you want, Gianni. That's life.'

'Oh yes, I understand now. But you will like me.'

'No.'

'I will give you reasons for to like me.'

Stephanie was losing her patience.

'Your English is clearly not as good as you think it is. You seem to be having trouble in understanding me.'

'No problem.'

'Really?'

'I understand.'

'Good. Then understand this. Go away, Gianni. I don't like you. I don't want you. Past tense, I did not like you. I did not want you. Future tense, I will not like you. I will not want you. Clear?'

'I like this.' He laughed loudly.

'Go away.'

'Yes, yes. I like this. You are very amusing.'

Suddenly, without warning, he leapt at her. He was fast on his feet but somewhere in the back of her mind Stephanie had had the feeling that he was going to do something like this and had kept herself alert. When his lunge came she executed a neat sidestep, leaving his grasping outstretched hand holding nothing more than her towel.

'I told you to get out.'

'You're so beautiful. I know you like me.' He was circling her now, the towel in his hand like a matador's cape. 'Please, I beg you. I know what you're like now. I want you so much.'

Stephanie assumed 'now' meant now that she was naked.

'This is very boring,' she said making no attempt to hide her naked body again.

'Please let me fuck you. Please.'

'No.'

'Yes. I will pay you.'

'I'm not a whore, Gianni.'

'One million lire.'

'No.' She had no idea how much one million lire was. 'Not for a million pounds.'

Gianni sat on the bed and pulled off his shirt, his socks and his shoes. He stood up and took off his trousers and the tiny black briefs he was wearing.

'I have a good body, yes?' He looked down at himself and breathed in.

Compared with Devlin his body was more athletic and more muscled but, of course, there was no comparison when it came to the cock that hung down between his legs, though even in its current semierect state it was by no means small.

Stephanie had no idea what to do next. She was not prepared to let this man have sex with her but, on the other hand, she didn't want to make him so cross he would take it out on Devlin and not do whatever deal he had been brought here to complete. Gianni was advancing towards her again, ready to lunge. She circled to the left. He moved to the left. She went right. He moved to the right which happened to be in the same direction as the bedroom door. Seeing the key in the lock, Gianni took the opportunity of locking the door, taking the key out and holding it up triumphantly, like a hunter bagging a lion.

'The key to paradise,' he said, grinning from ear to ear.

Stephanie retreated again. Gianni advanced. Then he lunged. This time, despite Stephanie's reflexes, she was not quite quick enough and he caught her by the wrist.

'Come on, Gianni, you don't want me this way, do you?' She let her wrist go limp in his hand.

'Anyway. You make me craz*ee*.'

'It would be rape.'

'No. You like me.'

His arrogance made it impossible for him to understand that a woman, any woman, would actually not want to sleep with him. He was just not capable of believing it.

He started to pull her towards him, reeling her in like a fish on a line. She could see his penis was beginning to harden, obviously excited by the prospect of coming into contact with her body at long last. As he pulled her in he released her wrist so that he could wrap his arms around her waist, but this was a mistake. As he snaked his arms around, she ducked out of the embrace and was free again. Backing away from him she suddenly realised that the bathroom door would lock from the inside. At least being trapped in the bathroom would be better than being raped by Gianni, and sooner or later Devlin would come looking for her. Fortunately, the bathroom door was nearer to her than it was to Gianni.

Gianni saw her escape route and knew he could not reach it before her. From having her in his arms she had now virtually escaped. Life was so unfair.

'Do you want me to beg? I beg, please, I beg?' He said it in his most pathetic voice.

But as he spoke he made one last despairing and, for him, disastrous effort, leaping forward with all his energy. Unfortunately the toes of one foot caught in the trailing edge of the bedspread which was fringed with an openworked crochet that effectively netted his toes. The force

97

of his leap carried him forward, for a split second suspended in midair a foot in front of Stephanie's startled face before his entrapped foot and gravity bought him crashing down to the floor, flat out on his stomach. As if this wasn't bad enough, in the various manoeuvres around the bedroom one of his shoes must have been kicked from where he had taken it off at the side of the bed to a position where now, as he fell, it was turned up and lying directly under his genitals. As he crashed to the floor his balls made contact with the rather large heel of the shoe. He screamed in agony, doubling up on the floor.

Stephanie tried not to laugh as he lay on the floor, every movement bringing another wave of pain. As he got his breath back the pain from his balls seemed to increase. There was pain from his toes too; he had broken at least one. And he'd fallen on his hand and now his wrist felt swollen.

Once Stephanie had managed to control her desire to laugh, she pulled on a robe and tried to help Gianni to his feet. He was not going to be a threat now, that was certain. The effort of getting up seemed to bring on more pain and he moaned in agony once again. He showed absolutely no interest in Stephanie and merely shook his head when she asked if he needed a doctor. Still naked and looking extremely sorry for himself, he limped out of the bedroom. He had tried to put on some of his clothes, but had discovered his swollen balls were too tender to tolerate being crammed into the tiny black briefs the sales assistant in Rome had assured him were the latest fashion.

Watching him struggle to unlock the bedroom door and then limp from the room, clothes slung over his arm, Stephanie only just managed not to laugh. But as the bedroom door closed, the effort proved too much for her and she collapsed on to the bed, rolling from side to side, tears of laughter streaming down her face. She recovered temporarily, enough to get to her feet, but the sight of Gianni's hapless shoe, still lying up-turned on the carpet, brought on another bout of helpless mirth.

Chapter Eight

The sun was well down on the horizon and the cool provided by the lengthening shadows was welcome. Stephanie, wearing the practical cotton dress she had travelled in, had been shown through a series of rooms, corridors and stairways to the other side of the castle, the side farthest from the lake. Now, from the top of a stone staircase, she surveyed the scene. Here stretching out for many miles she could see farmland, neat orchards – cherry and peach trees, she thought, certainly apple and pear – all impeccably kept. Nearer to the castle was about an acre of kitchen garden surrounded by an ageing red-brick wall. Inside the wall there were sheds and greenhouses as well as neatly arranged plant beds. She could see several men and women carrying out various gardening jobs, most on the north side of the compound where a small vineyard had been planted.

Dismissing the servants who had shown her through the maze of corridors, Stephanie walked down the steps, enjoying the cool breeze that blew lightly into her face. The air was heavily scented here too, this time from the climbing roses that had been used to decorate much of the wall of the garden. A tall wrought-iron gate surmounted by a brick arch led through the wall into the garden itself. Stephanie was in no particular hurry and wandered happily among the immaculately cultivated vegetables, the soft fruit bushes, the long rows of salad plants and the beds of flowers obviously intended to provide a constant supply of cut blooms for the castle. The rows were laid out with military precision, completely free of weeds, the result, she thought, of hundreds of hours of back-breaking manual labour.

She noticed a large modern greenhouse devoted to nothing but orchids and remembered the beautiful orchids Venetia had delivered to her with Devlin's compliments that night in London. So Devlin *had* grown them himself.

As she passed one or two of the labourers she thought she recognised a face or two from the cellars, but they kept their heads bowed and did not look up at her. They were all fully dressed in working clothes, which made them even less familiar. Among the neatly planted rows there were two or three figures dressed entirely in black. As they did little work themselves but wandered up and down watching the labourers, Stephanie imagined these were some sort of supervisors. She'd half expected them to be carrying whips.

It took Stephanie some minutes before she found the girl she was looking for. She was working on the vines pruning each vine back to the root. It was hard work and the girl was sweating profusely. As she approached her one of the supervisors, who had been watching her progress through the garden from the moment she had stepped through the gate, hurried forward.

'Can I help you?' he said. His English, though spoken with a strong Italian accent, was perfect, but his voice was high-pitched and reedy. Though he was clearly not mute, Stephanie couldn't help wondering if he had been a victim of the same 'accident' that had befallen Bruno.

'I need this girl in the castle.' The blonde looked around

to see if Stephanie was referring to her. 'You are English, aren't you?' she asked directly.

'Yes.'

'Yes, *madam*,' the supervisor corrected. The girl said nothing.

'Come with me, then,' Stephanie said.

For a second the supervisor looked as though he were going to intervene. Then he obviously thought better of it and stepped aside. Perhaps Devlin allowed other women the run of the castle, as he had Stephanie, and he was used to receiving orders from strangers; or perhaps it was just Stephanie's growing purposefulness and air of authority. What's more, she found she was continuing to enjoy this unaccustomed role that circumstances and Devlin had cast her in.

The girl pulled off her thick gardening gloves and dropped them with the pruning knife at the supervisor's feet. She knew that because of Stephanie's presence he would not tell her to pick them up. But Stephanie was not going to allow her to get away with open defiance.

'They don't belong there, do they?' Stephanie said firmly.

Once again the girl said nothing.

'Do they?'

'No,' she replied sullenly.

'Then put them back where they belong and then meet me by the gate.'

The supervisor looked pleased and the girl dejected as she stooped to pick up the gloves and knife.

Stephanie walked slowly over to the gate, watching the tall blonde return the things to a shed and then walk towards her. Her whole posture was defiant, as it had been in the cellars this morning. There was no question, too, that this woman was very beautiful. Even in the rough working clothes her natural grace and poise was obvious. She took off her scarf and shook her head to release her long blonde hair. She was not only beautiful; she was clearly very aware of it.

'So what's this all about, then?' she asked as she reached the gate. Her accent had a distinct Cockney twang to it and one she made no attempt to hide.

'Don't talk to me like that.'

'Why? Who do you think you are? Devlin's the boss here. You're just his tart for the day aren't you?'

'You could say that. It doesn't mean I can't get Bruno down here. Would you prefer it if I got him to bring you in?'

'No.' The mention of Bruno seemed to be effective.

'Good. Then you better follow me.'

Stephanie walked back into the castle, the blonde following morosely but without further comment. Clearly Stephanie was going to have to think of something to get her to cooperate over dinner. If she remained as sulky and ill-tempered as she was now, Gianni was going to be about as turned on as a man standing out in a snowstorm. There was no question of her beauty. If she could only find a way to make her more pliant, Gianni would surely be as excited by her as he was by Stephanie. Then she remembered what Devlin had said about trying to make the punishment fit the crime. She could always promise to reduce the girl's 'sentence' at the castle. As Devlin was so desperate to please Gianni, she was sure he would not raise any objections.

When they finally got back to Stephanie's room after the long journey through the seemingly endless corridors of the castle, Stephanie poured the champagne she had ordered before she left, into two glasses that stood by the wine cooler. She offered one to the girl.

'Can I shower first? I'm filthy.'

'Good idea. The bathroom's over there.'

The girl disappeared into the bathroom but did not close

the door after her. Stephanie heard the sound of the shower. She sipped at her champagne then walked into the bathroom. The blonde was standing with her face under the stream of water. As she saw Stephanie she turned around to face her, as if to show off her naked body – almost, again, as an act of defiance. Water ran down over her breasts, into her thick blonde pubic hair, then over her long thighs. Her body was as perfect as her face. Her breasts were not large but they were firm and round with dark puckered nipples. Her thighs were muscled, long and shapely with no excess fat, and then curved in at her crotch so that now, even as she stood with her legs together, there was a clear channel between them. Her buttocks were a natural extension of her long legs, not large and fleshy, but taut and pert, arching out in a sharp curve from the small of her back.

Stephanie realised she was not looking objectively at this body. Her pulse had quickened with the excitement of desire. She thought of Venetia. She thought of her experience with Dolly.

'What's your name?' The girl was wearing a name tag that read *Linda*.

'We are not allowed . . .'

'What you're not allowed to do doesn't seem to bother you much so far.'

'Colette.'

'And I'm Stephanie.'

Colette stepped out of the shower and turned off the water. She seemed completely unembarrassed by her nakedness. Or was it something else? Was she using her nakedness to try to provoke a reaction in Stephanie? A sexual reaction? Towelling herself dry, Colette sat on the loo. Stephanie heard her pee.

'Come out on the terrace when you've finished,' she said.

Stephanie carried the champagne glasses out on to the

terrace. The air was pleasantly cool in the lengthening shade and the view of the lake as the sun hung low in the sky was, yet again, miraculous. Gianni had undoubtedly cast a shadow over the weekend but Stephanie was determined not to let him spoil everything. If she could persuade Colette to cooperate she could relieve Devlin's obvious preoccupation with making Gianni happy. Devlin, for whatever reason, was more worried than he was saying, of that Stephanie was certain, and his anxiety centred on Gianni. Whatever the contract Gianni was here to sign, it was clearly terribly important to Devlin.

Colette stepped out on to the terrace, a short towel wrapped around her breasts, covering her down to the top of her thighs and leaving her long legs exposed. Stephanie glimpsed the thick mat of pubic hair, now dry and fluffy. Colette came over to the table and picked up her glass of champagne, drinking it thirstily. She put out her hand and stroked the side of Stephanie's black hair.

'If you want to fuck me it's not a problem, darling,' she said, looking straight into Stephanie's eyes. 'You only have to say the word.'

The excitement Stephanie had felt in the bathroom returned. She would have loved to take this magnificent creature to her bed and lose herself in her body as she had done with Venetia's back in London. But, she quickly reminded herself, at the moment there were other priorities.

'Sit down.'

'Is that an order, madam?' Colette said mockingly, sitting down nevertheless. Stephanie sat beside her at the table.

'How long have you been here?'

'Two weeks.'

'What did you do?'

'You know that, don't you?'

'You worked for Devlin?'

'Indirectly. I worked for one of the companies he owns.'

105

'Doing what?'

'Import-export.'

'And you got caught with your hand in the till?'

'Yes.'

'Tell me more. I'm interested.'

Colette told her story in level unemotional tones, seemingly showing no remorse for her act but only regret at having been caught. Several of the customers of the import side of the business in England had wanted preferential treatment on a particular line of goods that were selling like hot cakes and were in short supply. Colette diverted the goods that did reach England to these customers, who were able to make a handsome profit by selling them off at higher prices, instead of sharing them equally to all. In return she received a large kickback. Unfortunately, the other customers of the company were very unhappy at what was going on. Some of them had been supplied by Devlin's firm for many years and could not understand why they were being treated so badly. It did not take long for their complaints to prompt an investigation by an expert in company security who easily discovered Colette's involvement.

'I was told to report to an office in Mayfair,' Colette continued, taking another sip of champagne. 'I had no idea why. I had no idea who Devlin was. He told me that I had been caught defrauding the company. He showed me the proof. They had it all — invoices, my bank statements, everything. He said it was a very serious offence and they would press for the maximum sentence, which was seven years.'

'And?' Stephanie asked.

'Devlin told me I had an alternative to his going straight to the police with all the evidence. He told me about this place. He told me that I was a very beautiful and desirable woman and that if I came to the castle as a ...' she hesitated.

'Slave?'

'Yes. Well, if I did that the evidence would be destroyed and I'd be free.'

'For how long?'

'Twenty-six weeks.'

Stephanie could not help a whistle of surprise. Devlin had said six months was the maximum. 'You must have cost him a lot of money.'

'I did.' For the first time a smile crossed Colette's face.

'So you agreed?'

'Being here is better than prison, isn't it?'

'You don't seem to remember that very often.'

'I remember it when it counts.'

'Well, I've got a proposition for you.'

'You don't have to threaten me to get what you want.'

'I'll get Devlin to let you leave in twenty weeks.'

'In exchange for what? If you want to fuck me, just say so. I'll do a good job. I like it.'

'That's not what I want.' Well, not at the moment, Stephanie thought.

'Pity. You're very attractive. It would have been a pleasure.'

'I want you to charm an Italian over dinner tonight. Really charm him. Make him want you.'

'That's all?'

'Just get him off my back.'

'And let him have his wicked way with me?'

'Let him do anything he wants with you.'

'But he can have me in the cellars. Anyway he wants. Whether I like it or not. You know that.'

'Shall we say he requires a more subtle approach. He wants to feel he's made a conquest.'

'So I've got to pretend to be a free agent?'

'Exactly.'

'Fifteen weeks.'

'Nineteen.'

'Eighteen.'

'All right. Eighteen.'

'I'll need some clothes. And underwear. And make-up.'

'I've got everything you need.'

Colette suddenly reached out and touched Stephanie's shoulder.

'How much time do we have?'

'Enough.'

'Could we go to bed first? You're so attractive, Stephanie. You turn me on. I haven't had a woman since I've been here. I think Devlin knows that's what I'm into. He's very clever about these things.' Her hand slipped down to Stephanie's breast and squeezed it gently. 'Don't tell me you don't want it. I could see by the way you looked at me in the bathroom.'

'No . . .' Stephanie said with no conviction.

'Yes . . .' Colette said strongly. 'Have you got a dildo? I love being fucked with a dildo. They go so deep. Really fill you up. Then I could lick you. I'm very good at that. I know just where to lick. Only a woman knows . . .'

'Stop it.'

Colette's hand was still working on Stephanie's breast.

'Why? If I touched you now you'd be wet wouldn't you?' Colette's hand slipped into Stephanie's lap and started to pull up the material of her skirt inch by inch. 'I bet you're hot too.'

Stephanie grasped her wrist.

'If you're not wet I'll stop.' The hand was poised on Stephanie's knickers now. Colette's fingers probed down between her legs. 'You see,' she said. The knickers were hot and damp.

'Don't,' Stephanie pleaded, but so softly Colette did not hear what she said.

'You're so hot, so wet.' Colette was standing over her

now sawing her finger up and down the little white crotch of the knickers. 'I'm wet too.'

She pulled the towel off her body. Her nipples were hard. She put her own hand down into the thick thatch of pubic hair and found the opening of her cunt.

'You see? All for you,' she said, extracting a wet finger from between her legs and licking it hungrily.

For the whole time on the island Stephanie had been the dominant one. Even last night, spreadeagled on the bed by the two men, she had known that she was in control of the situation. Now, as Colette took her hand and led her into the bedroom, she felt, for the first time, submissive. She wanted this beautiful woman to control her, to take her, to be in charge. She stood by the bed and let Colette unbutton her dress, making no attempt to help her or hinder her. She was completely passive, wanting only to surrender herself. She let Colette pull the dress off her body, unhook her bra and tug her knickers to the floor. She let her press her back on to the bed and suck voraciously at her nipples, biting them, hurting them even while her hand kneaded the firm flesh of the breast. She made no attempt to open her legs. Colette had to lever them apart as she moved her head down over Stephanie's flat stomach. When Stephanie's cunt was exposed Colette dipped her head down between Stephanie's legs and lapped at her cunt through the curly black hair as though she wanted to lick up all her juices. Stephanie lay there, making no attempt to reciprocate. She wanted to be used.

Stephanie's first orgasm was muted, brought on by the gentle but insistent rhythm of Colette's tongue on her clitoris. For some reason she suppressed her moan of pleasure. The sensations felt remote, as if the ripples of pleasure were being felt by some other body not related to hers.

She had no idea where Colette found the dildo. Perhaps all the castle bedrooms were equipped with such things.

She neither knew nor cared. She knew only that she loved the feeling that it produced as the cold hard plastic was driven mercilessly into her cunt. The feeling of remoteness disappeared. Colette's gentleness was gone too. She was using the dildo like a man's cock, forcing it home to the hilt. Stephanie's second orgasm was stronger, harder, produced by the hard dildo ramming into her ceaselessly while Colette's finger wanked at her clitoris. The second orgasm belonged to her, the feelings intense and centred. But she did not want a third.

'No more,' she said closing her legs and making Colette pull the dildo away.

Colette lay back on the bed and pushed the dildo, glistening with juices from Stephanie's cunt, deep into her own body. Using both her hands she pushed it as far up as it would go, arching her back off the bed, pointing herself at Stephanie so Stephanie could see every detail as the dildo plunged in and out. She writhed on the bed, squirming down on the hard plastic to get it just where she instinctively wanted it. Freeing one hand she pinched viciously at her own nipple, then wanked her clitoris. Her orgasm started to overwhelm her, spreading out from the top of her cunt through her body to her nipples and clitoris until it rocked every nerve she possessed. But more than any feelings the dildo produced it was, Colette knew, the look in Stephanie's eyes as she watched, riveted, Colette's masturbation that made her climax explode.

They decided on the red dress. It was strapless, tight and short, clinging to every inch of Colette's body, showing off her faultless figure and long legs, the red a perfect complement to Colette's blonde hair. It had taken them some time to decide on this dress from the selection they had found in the wardrobes of the bedroom next to Stephanie's. How many thousands of pounds worth of designer dresses, most admittedly evening dresses, hung in these wardrobes Stephanie dared not imagine. She had not been able to resist the temptation to try one or two for herself.

For a while the two women had been like young children let loose in a toy shop. Parading in front of mirrors in one exotic *haute couture* creation after another, matching shoes, and little evening bags, which they had also discovered in large numbers. But in the end Stephanie had not changed her mind about what she was going to wear – the dark blue dress Devlin had provided in London – and the tight red dress was definitely the most alluring for Colette. It presented a problem however. The material was too tight and clinging to wear anything underneath it. Even the briefest G-string would show. And stockings and suspenders were definitely out. Colette was quite happy to wear nothing but Stephanie insisted she would not look her best without something on her legs. Tights seemed the only answer and not a very satisfactory one. There was something distinctly work-a-day and unappealing about tights, Stephanie knew, however shiny and sheer they were.

It was Colette who discovered the solution. In one of the drawers of the wardrobes, as packed with designer underwear as the hanging rails were with dresses, she found packs of crotchless tights. They were very sheer and fine with a superb, almost shimmering lustre, but around the area between the legs a carefully seamed oval shape had been removed, leaving the whole crotch exposed. Colette had quickly tried them on and Stephanie had to admit they were surprisingly sexy. Somehow the fact that so much of the leg and backside was covered in silky sheer nylon made the crotch itself seem more exposed and available.

With the red dress on, its skirt covering no more than a few inches of Colette's long thighs, these tights could not help but offer tantalising glimpses of what lay naked underneath, as tantalising, Stephanie hoped sincerely, as the tautly suspended black stockings that her skirt would undoubtedly and occasionally reveal.

Back in her own room, leaving Colette to apply the finishing touches to her make-up, Stephanie fastened the dark blue suspender belt around her slim waist and sat on the bed to pull the black stockings on. Pointing her toe she watched the material sheath her flesh, like a thick liquid painted on from between her hands. She clipped the suspenders into the welt of the stockings back and front and adjusted the straps so the stockings were held taut, pulling the nylon into little triangles on the smooth skin of her thigh. She stepped into the matching silk teddy, pulling its thin spaghetti straps over her shoulders and clipping together the three studs down between legs that held the silk of the crotch in place.

She sat at the dressing table and went to work on her make-up and hair. Looking at Colette in the red dress and tights she couldn't imagine that Gianni would be less than enthralled. Or was she being too optimistic? She could have quite easily thrown Colette on to a bed herself and continued where they had just left off. Surely Gianni would feel the same? She did not apply her make-up as heavily as she had the night before.

Her experience with Colette, and with Dolly this morning, she thought, as she applied her eye-liner with a steady hand, did not alarm her in the least. She had no feeling that she was beginning to want women more than men. Before she had met Venetia, Martin had arranged, at her own explicit request, her first experience with a woman. It had excited her. It had thrilled her. But it had been part of a *ménage à trois*. The experience with Venetia had been different. They had been alone, one on one. She had realised then that a woman was capable of giving her as much sexual pleasure as a man. It was a different pleasure, of course, and in the end not as satisfying, but an enormous pleasure nevertheless. What Colette had confirmed this afternoon, especially the desire and excitement she had felt at seeing Colette's magnificent body in the bathroom, and like the desire she had felt for Dolly, was that women were not just a passing phase in her sexuality. They were, and would be, a permanent feature.

With this and the discovery of her enjoyment of dominance and power, her weekend had become a voyage of self-discovery. She had explored new islands of feeling. They were islands that lay beyond her known world; new territory unmapped and lying in uncharted waters.

A few minutes ago, in the next-door bedroom, Colette had paraded in the short red dress. She had bent down to pick up a discarded shoe and Stephanie had seen the whole of the long slit of her sex exposed and framed by the tights, from the little puckered hole in her arse to the pulpy labia amply covered by the thick pubic hair. It was a sight that had provoked a rush of visceral pleasure in Stephanie. But that did not mean she was not equally excited, for instance, by the sight of Devlin's cock ramming deep into her cunt as she had bent over the bath, or of the masked man on the plane, his cock straining for the release she had, eventually, given him.

The truth was, she knew, as she applied lipstick with a brush, that she wanted it all. She wanted the fantasies and the realities. She wanted men and women. She wanted dominance and she wanted submission. She had stumbled into a world of sex that she had only ever read about before, and it had thrilled her. She could not believe her body capable of producing the depth of feelings, the heights of passion she had already experienced. For whatever reason, at this moment in her life, she was completely receptive to this new sexual domain into which she had wandered. She did not fear it, she was not inhibited by it, she was not in any straitjacket of psychological repressions or suppressions. There was nothing holding her back. There was nothing between her and her feelings.

Why then, she thought, had she resisted Gianni so vehemently? To have a man who she disliked and despised, who made her flesh creep (ever-so-slightly creep, she had to admit) take her and fuck her would be another island of feeling to explore. She would feel used, abused. Would it be so different from the other experiences she had already willingly encountered?

For the moment the answer was definitely yes. Despite all that had happened the thought of Gianni did not provoke the slightest sexual arousal. He was quite simply a turn-off. How long that feeling would last she did not know, but at the moment it was a fact.

As she pulled the dark blue evening dress over the teddy Colette walked back into the room. The transformation from the sweaty labourer toiling in the vineyards to a beautiful and sophisticated creature was complete. Making no concessions to her height she had selected high-heeled shoes to match the dress. She had pinned her hair up to leave her long neck and shoulders completely bare, making the strapless dress seem even more revealing. Her firm breasts were clearly outlined by the clinging scarlet fabric, as was the curve of her arse.

'Well?' she said turning a full circle in front of Stephanie.

'Stunning,' Stephanie replied and meant it.

Stephanie smoothed down her own dress and went to stand by Colette. They gazed into the long full-length mirror. The skirt of Stephanie's dress was longer than Colette's but the split skirt, cleverly designed to be hidden until movement of the thigh caused it to open, made it no less attractive. The dress was tight to the waist following the line of her breasts but styled to cover one shoulder while leaving the other exposed. They were the perfect combination: blonde in red, brunette in blue, two stunningly attractive women dressed to the nines.

But something was missing, Stephanie decided as she looked at Colette in the mirror. Going through the small amount of jewellery she had brought with her, she found a gold necklace and clipped it into place around Colette's neck. The effect accentuated the graceful hollows above her collarbone. Stephanie chose only earrings for herself.

'Let's go then,' she said.

'What happens if this doesn't work?'

'Your guess is as good as mine,' Stephanie said, knowing it to be true. Stephanie would have preferred to be going down to dinner with Devlin alone. Gianni's presence was intrusive, but, she had to admit, it also added an extra dimension of excitement and interest. There was definitely no way to predict how this evening was going to end.

Chapter Nine

The clack of high heels on the marble staircase must have alerted Devlin and Gianni. By the time the two women were halfway down the stairs, both men were standing at the foot of the staircase waiting to greet them. From this position there was no doubt they were getting a worm's eye view of two pairs of unrivalled legs expensively clad in nylon and leather. In Colette's case they could probably see a great deal more.

'Bravo! Bravo!' Gianni shouted, beginning to clap his hands. Devlin rather self-consciously joined in.

'Magnificent,' Devlin said quietly to Stephanie as she reached the bottom of the stairs and he took her hand.

'Thank you,' she replied. She turned to Gianni.

'This is Colette, a friend of mine from England,' she lied.

'Charmed, Colette,' Gianni said taking her hand and kissing it lasciviously, no doubt using the same technique he had used on Stephanie on the jetty. 'I love English. Did Stephanie tell you? All things English. I'm English-*crazee*.'

He was looking hard at Stephanie as he said this, looking at her, it seemed, as though he saw straight through her little plot.

'And there's something about Italian men makes me feel

funny in all sorts of places,' Colette was saying, her Cockney accent suddenly more pronounced.

Gianni turned to Stephanie and took her hand. He kissed it perfunctorily, letting it go as soon as his lips had grazed the skin of her fingers.

'To you I must owe an apology. I behave very badly indeed. Please I want that you forgive me.'

'Forgiven and forgotten,' Stephanie said catching Devlin's eye. Whether this change of mind was genuine or not she did not know. But at least he'd said it. And it was possible that he meant it.

'Good. Then we can be friends,' he said.

Gianni wrapped his arm around Colette's waist and led her into the dining room, his hand quickly slipping down from the small of her back to the cheeks of her arse, feeling them move as she walked.

'Well, that's a good sign,' Stephanie whispered to Devlin.

'So far, so good. She looks stunning.'

'Do you want her?'

'My dear, I want only you. This business has spoilt all my plans. I didn't want to have to share you this evening. I wanted you to myself. Will you ever forgive me?'

'I might.' She tried to look stern but then broke into a smile. Two pleas for forgiveness in as many minutes. 'Incidentally, I had to promise her ...'

'Anything. If she can get Gianni out of our hair, anything.'

'I have something special for our aperitif,' Devlin announced as when they were installed in chairs around the roaring fire in the dining room. 'A bottle of 1952 Dom Perignon.'

A white-coated waiter poured the wine into the flutes, handling the bottle as though it contained nitro-glycerine. The wine had lost most of its bubbles but had matured to a deep golden colour.

'To our mutual health,' Devlin toasted.

Stephanie could not remember tasting anything so delicious. She savoured the subtle taste, sipping the wine from the flute and watching Devlin do the same.

'Delicious.'

'It's the last bottle, and I've been saving it for a special occasion,' he said, looking only at Stephanie.

Gianni and Colette were less judicious, gulping back the wine as if it were Coca-Cola.

'How long have you been friends?' Gianni asked in a tone Stephanie thought was edged with suspicion.

'Oh, years . . .' Stephanie lied.

'But you talk differently.'

'I'm a Cockney, see.' Colette volunteered.

'But you are both beautiful. It is very unusual to have two beautiful women as friends. Usually it is one beautiful and one very ugly. The horse and the donkey. No?'

'Doesn't he say the nicest things?' Colette said, leaning over to kiss Gianni's cheek while her hand pawed his thigh.

'Well,' Devlin said, trying to change the subject, 'dinner is served.'

Devlin led Stephanie to the dining table. It was now set for four. A huge display of fresh flowers – obviously from the kitchen garden – decorated the centre of the table. Gianni sat next to Colette, facing Stephanie; Devlin next to Stephanie facing Colette. Before them a vast array of crystal glasses and Georg Jensen silver arranged neatly in place settings. Stephanie realised that she was ravenously hungry, having eaten nothing since the light lunch on the terrace. She accepted the proffered bread – there was a choice of three and Stephanie chose the rough country bread Devlin recommended – with alacrity, while another waiter offered mineral water which she also accepted.

'In Gianni's honour tonight we have Italian specialities,' Devlin said of the meal he had planned so carefully for

Stephanie. '*Pasta nero* with white truffles from Alba. Our local fish from the lake deep-fried *misto fritto*. And local veal roasted in wild rosemary with polenta. There is a dolcelatta from Bologna and a special pudding. All guaranteed to have no calories whatsoever.'

No wonder there were so many knives and forks on the table, Stephanie thought. It was not until her first taste of white truffle, thinly pared on to the black pasta and accompanied by a fine Frascati, that she realised her intimations of trouble were well founded. The first sign was a shoe, rubbing gently against the top of her ankle. Looking down through the glass table top it was not difficult to see to whom the shoe belonged. It was one of Gianni's Gucci loafers. Gianni himself was talking to Devlin, apparently oblivious to what his foot was up to. Colette had seen what was going on too. The women looked at each other over the table. Colette shrugged. She was doing her best. Stephanie withdrew her foot to a point where it was out of Gianni's reach. She watched as his foot searched around, probing like the antenna of an ant, trying to re-establish contact. Finally he gave up, though not without giving Stephanie a quick glance and a knowing smile.

Course followed course, each perfectly cooked, each accompanied by a different classic Italian wine. Gianni ate greedily, stuffing the food into his mouth as though he hadn't eaten for weeks and using the wine, rather than the water, to wash it all down. Gianni's wine glass seemed to be perpetually empty, despite being refilled by a succession of conscientious waiters. And the alcohol was clearly affecting him. The veneer of politeness he had adopted to Stephanie at the beginning of the evening and the apparent interest in Colette was wearing thin. He was staring at Stephanie all the time now, no matter who he was talking to. He winked at her. He put his hand across the table to touch hers. His foot snaked out to touch hers the moment she inadvertently brought it back into range. Whatever Colette had, Gianni did not want it; that was becoming patently obvious. As the meal progressed the frown on Devlin's forehead deepened. There was seemingly nothing that could be done to drag Gianni's attention away from Stephanie and on to Colette. The plan was not working.

The special pudding was an amazing concoction of chocolate and cream and almond biscuits, but it went largely uneaten except by Gianni, who cleaned his plate of every morsel and then looked over at the amount left on Stephanie's plate.

'You are leaving this?' he asked, sounding astonished.

'Yes.'

'Do you mind? It's too good for wasting.' His fork flashed out over the table and scooped up most of the pudding from Stephanie's plate leaving a trail of cream and chocolate, dropped from his ambitiously filled spoon, between her plate and his.

'Colette has some left,' Devlin said hopefully, but Gianni was not interested in what Colette had on her plate.

'I want only Stephanie's,' he said, flamboyantly throwing her a kiss across the table.

'I'm hurt,' Colette said, pouting her bottom lip in a manner that most men in her life had found irresistible.

'No, no, my dear.' Gianni put his arm around her bare shoulder and patted her arm. 'You must excuse. I have eaten that much enough.'

'No,' Colette continued trying her best. 'I'm hurt. What are are going to do to make it up to me?'

'What can I do?'

'Well, I can think of a little something ...' She leant forward and whispered in his ear. But whatever she said did not produce the desired effect.

'No, no!' Gianni said like a petulant child whose toy was

being taken away from him for bad behaviour. 'I want to stay with my friends.'

Colette caught Stephanie's eye and gave her a resigned look. What more could she do?

They took coffee out on the terrace. The full moon had come out and was perfectly reflected in the still black water of the lake. The temperature was perfect, a balmy evening after a burningly hot day. Stephanie stood alone looking over the silent water. In daylight it was probably the most beautiful view she had ever seen. Now, at night, with the great white moon, it seemed a more emotional experience, as though the view signified something she should know and understand. As her eyes became accustomed to the darkness she could see faint lights in the far distance from the houses dotted around the edge of the lake. Moths and fireflies flew into the light from the lamps on the terrace. Apart from their frenzied suicidal fluttering the night was completely still.

Colette had taken Gianni's arm and forcefully steered him to a small outdoor couch. His interest in her seemed to have been rekindled.

'You're the sort of man that makes me feel ... well, hot. I mean turned on. There's something about you. Something like an animal ... do you know what I mean?' Her hand pressed into his lap, her fingers actively searching for his cock. 'I don't usually feel like this. Men are all over me usually and I don't want to know. But with you ... do you know what I mean?'

'You are a beautiful creature.' Gianni meant it, too. She was exquisite.

'I'm glad you think so.' Her fingers had found their objective. 'I hope you don't think I do this all the time. It's just something you do to me. Maybe it's your Eyetie accent ...'

'Maybe. You have a beautiful body too, I think.'

'I just have this feeling, see. Makes me all funny inside. I just know what it would be like with you. I don't think I'd be able to control myself. You'd make me wild, Gianni.'

Tentatively Gianni put his hand on her knee. The sheer nylon felt soft and warm to his touch and he felt Colette shudder slightly and let out the faintest of moans. He ran his hand higher up her leg. Her legs parted.

'Oh, that's so nice. You don't know how good that feels.'

'Your legs are so long.'

He ran his fingertips down between her thighs and then higher until he could have sworn he felt the brush of hair against the side of his hand. He investigated further, turning his fingertips inward and discovering that the nylon did not extend over her thick bushy pubic hair. Colette meantime was squeezing his cock which was beginning to grow.

'Clever design, isn't it?' she whispered. 'Nothing to get in the way. It's making you hard, isn't it? Tell me what you want, darling . . .' Colette was increasingly pleased with herself. At last her charms were working. 'Anything. As long as you fuck me first. I'll do anything. Tell me your fantasy, Gianni.'

Gianni was more than tempted. She was a beautiful creature. He looked down at the red dress, the material moulded to her breasts, and at her sculpted, slender thighs. He knew he could ask her anything and she would do it. He wished he didn't care, didn't care that Devlin was treating him like a fool, taking him for a complete idiot. But he did care and he knew himself too well to be tempted for long. In the end where would he be, how would he feel, how could he look at himself in the mirror in the morning if he took this girl to his bed, a girl like any whore he could buy on the streets of Rome? More beautiful perhaps, more skilled even, but no more than a common whore nevertheless.

'That's enough.' He stood up.

'Darling!' Colette said with genuine surprise as her hand was torn away from his cock.

'What do you take me for?' Gianni strode over to the table where Stephanie and Devlin sat with their coffee. 'Hah, Devlin, what you take me for?'

'What's the problem?' Devlin said, trying to sound unconcerned.

'This girl. You think I'm stupid. You set me up with a whore. You think I need to fuck a whore?'

'Gianni . . .' Devlin was lost for words.

'Get her out of here.' He looked back at Colette. Her skirt had ridden up on the sofa and a wisp of pubic hair, as blonde as the hair on her head, curled up from beneath the red hem of the dress. 'I don't go with whores, Devlin. I told you this. What, you bring her up from your cellars, eh? Your famous cellars. You think I don't know all about you? You think I don't find out all about you? I don't need this. I get my own women. I never take a whore.'

'She's my friend,' Stephanie said.

'She is not. Don't lie to me.' He spat the words out at her with real hate.

Devlin got to his feet and took Gianni by the arm. Gianni shook his hand off but followed him into the castle. At the terrace doors he turned and shot a look back at the women. His eyes blazed with anger.

'What did you say to him?' Stephanie asked, sitting down next to Colette on the couch.

'I was just trying to get him going. It was no good, though. He knew from the beginning, right from the off. He just played along. He was never interested in me. He wants you and that's it.'

'I know,' Stephanie sighed.

'I did what I could.'

'It's not your fault.'

Through the windows Stephanie could see Gianni

123

pacing up and down the dining room angrily gesticulating at Devlin. Devlin was clearly trying to calm him down. Stephanie felt miserable. What was supposed to be a romantic dinner had been turned into a shambles by this awful man, the whole evening had been spent trying to placate him. She knew nothing of Devlin's business but, considering his enormous wealth, whatever Devlin wanted from him must be very important indeed. She just wished it did not involve her.

Devlin opened the door on to the terrace.

'Colette,' he called, for all the world like a headmaster summoning an errant pupil into his study.

Colette glanced at Stephanie, shrugged her shoulders and walked into the castle through the open terrace door. Devlin closed the door behind her, pointedly not looking at Stephanie.

Perhaps she should walk in and tell Gianni he could have her, fuck her, do whatever he pleased with her. Would it be too much to ask? After all that had happened at the castle it wouldn't take much effort on her part, and it would undoubtedly help Devlin to get Gianni to concentrate on the deal they were supposed to be doing. But she was in no mood to make such a gesture. She was angry with Devlin. He had invited her here. He had promised her a wonderful weekend and she, for her part, had given as good as she got. But from the point that Gianni stepped out of the boat – actually from the time Devlin had taken his telephone call – it had been downhill all the way. If she drew the line at sleeping with a man she despised, and his performance at dinner had done nothing to change her mind about him, she saw no reason to reproach herself with that. She should not be apologising to Devlin for her actions; he should be apologising to her. Devlin seemed to have forgotten everything in his headlong desire to please Gianni at whatever cost.

Through the long terrace window Stephanie watched Devlin talking to Colette, who seemed to be shaking her head to refuse whatever he was suggesting. Gianni, his face twisted with anger, took her by the arm, wrenching her round to face him while he shouted something at her. Stephanie could see Colette's skin go white where Gianni gripped her arm. Her head started to nod in reluctant agreement, and Gianni let her go and, with a parting gesture to Devlin which Stephanie could not understand, stormed out of the room.

Devlin took Colette's arm now, but more gently. He talked to her calmly and then both of them moved out of sight.

It was some minutes before the terrace door opened again and Colette stepped out, carrying a tray with a bottle of brandy and three large brandy glasses.

'Devlin thought you'd need a drink.'

'Where is he?'

'He's trying to calm Gianni down. He'll be out in a minute.'

'What was all that about?'

'Oh, just having a go at me,' she lied, avoiding Stephanie's eyes. She poured the brandy and handed Stephanie a glass. 'It's not my fault, Stephanie.'

'I know. You did your best.'

'I'm sorry,' she said with genuine feeling.

Devlin was right. Stephanie felt like a large drink and took a good belt of the brandy. She did not notice that Colette made no attempt to drink from her glass. She just wanted Devlin to come back so they could salvage what was left of the evening. Maybe she could suggest to him that they take Colette up to her room and find ways of forgetting this awful man. She would love to have Colette and Devlin together. His enormous fingers and cock, her long legs, soft mouth and thick thatch of pubic hair. The combinations of delight would be endless. She could tease out Colette's clitoris while Devlin fucked her; she could suck it and lick it and lose herself in it.

A funny thing was happening to the moon. Instead of being round it was melting. All its white centre was melting and pouring itself into the lake like an old advertisement for milk chocolate. A glass and a half in every bar pouring into the chocolate lake. She'd wished she'd eaten the chocolate pudding. It was so delicious. Fresh chocolate from the chocolate lake. But the moon was melting away and it was getting darker and darker as it disappeared. Even the lights on the terrace, round balls of light, were melting away, pouring down on to the ceramic tiled paving. All that light melting away. It was so dark ...

She could hardly see Colette now. She was standing right next to her she knew but even in that beautiful red dress she couldn't see her. She'd have liked to be able to see her so she could pull down the front of the strapless dress, pull it down over her breasts leaving them naked, and pull up the skirt over those clever tights that left everything exposed and available. She'd like to have sunk her teeth into those hard nipples, sunk her fingers into that soft hairy cunt, buck her own pubic bone against Colette's as though fucking her, pretending she had a cock. But she could hardly see her it was so dark and what she could see was melting away too just like the moon and the terrace lamps. The large red splotch of colour that was all she could make out of Colette was melting away, pouring into the terrace paving until it had completely disappeared and it was dark. She was all on her own and it was completely dark, pitch black all round her. Not that she was frightened. She felt warm and relaxed and happy. She sang a little song to herself. She lay back on the sofa and sang a little song all to herself.

When she stopped singing she could hear voices but she did not understand what they were saying.

'That was quick.' It was Devlin's voice.

'She drank it quickly. Why are you doing this?'

'Please remember who you are, Colette,' he said sternly. 'Do you actually think I want to do this?'

'Why don't you just tell him to go to hell?'

'Because the contract would go with him.'

'She promised me . . .'

'Whatever she promised you I'll deliver. Now go and get Bruno to carry her downstairs.'

'Is he so important?'

'Yes,' Devlin said. 'And now he's got what he wants, hasn't he?'

Stephanie gave up the effort to find meaning in these conversations and relaxed. It didn't matter. She let her mind drift to delicious thoughts of Venetia, and Colette, and Devlin. Somewhere in the back of her mind she realised she hadn't mentioned Venetia to Devlin. She would. She'd get round to it. Meantime she felt too good to worry about anything. She thought she felt herself being lifted but as her whole body felt as if it was completely weightless and floating it was impossible to tell for sure. And anyway the temptation to close her eyes – or were they already closed? It was so dark – and let herself fall into the billowing clouds of sleep engulfing her was too much to resist.

The dream was not vivid, not like the sort of dream where everything is so vivid it's difficult to believe it's not real. This dream had only feelings and emotions and sensations. Stephanie could not tell where she was. She knew she was naked but she could not see her body. She *felt* naked. And she knew her body was being manipulated, expertly handled and touched and explored. She felt herself being caressed and kissed. She felt lips sucking at her nipples, she felt fingers circling her clitoris, and then the soft wetness of a hot tongue licking her clitoris before plunging deeper between her legs and pushing into her cunt itself, deeper than she'd ever felt a tongue before. Everything was perfect, every touch exactly what she would have wanted, no need to ask for anything, no need to interfere. Everything she'd dreamt she'd wanted from a lover, this lover was doing in her dream.

After his hands and tongue had probed and touched her weightless body – she knew instinctively it was a 'he' – her legs were opened and she arched her back to present herself to this phantom. Then she felt cock, hard and hot, pressing into her, filling her, taking advantage of the expert preparations. In her dream she knew it was not Devlin's cock. This was a dream cock, the perfect cock, fitting her cunt exactly as she'd dreamt a cock should do, nudging all the right places, the whole cock inside her so she could feel her clitoris grinding against the very base of it as it started an insistent tempo. Out almost all the way, until she could feel the heat of its tip between her swollen labia and then back in again, buffeting the very top of her womb and the knot of her clitoris at the same time. On and on and on. She felt no physical exertion. She felt only the sensation of sex, her whole body reduced to the feelings from her cunt.

She could feel her orgasm. It was not sharp and quick but part of a dream, long and slow and intense. It was like a dam about to burst. Every stroke of his cock building the pressure of the water against the dam, knowing the dam would burst, watching its structure crumble away, knowing it was inevitable but somehow wanting to hold back for as long as possible. At the same time she could feel his pressure growing too, the dam inside his cock about to burst, the pressure from his spunk building until it would be too great to resist. His cock was swelling inside her, filling with spunk. She could feel his spunk, feel it hot and white waiting for release.

Her orgasm broke the dam, surrounded and enclosed her. She could feel nothing but the cock inside her and her body's reaction to it. In her dream she could see the cock, see it pushing up between the folds of flesh in her cunt, pushing for release. As she felt his cock jerk and spasm inside her she could see the little oval slit in his glans open and shoot spunk deep into her, pulse after pulse of white spunk. And that completed her orgasm, burst through the last stones of the dam, and she felt herself drowning in a sea of sexual ecstasy, wet with spunk and cunt juice and emotion. It was the perfect orgasm, in a perfect dream.

She wanted to thank him now. But she couldn't find him. She was looking for him knowing he was still there but she couldn't find him. Where had he gone? She searched and then, somewhere in the distance she saw him. Immediately she felt a rush of excitement. They could do it all over again. Burst the dams again. Feel and touch and suck and fuck again. That's what she wanted. Desperately wanted. This man had given her so much pleasure.

She was running towards him. She could see him clearly and in her mind she knew she recognised him. She knew him. He was fully dressed but had his back to her. She stood behind him and she heard herself telling him that she had never had such beautiful sex, that he'd made her feel wonderful, alive, open. But he still didn't turn round.

'Kiss me,' she heard herself saying.

She took him by the shoulder and he turned round. In the dream he turned in slow motion. He turned and lifted her into his arms and kissed her full on the mouth and she kissed him back hard with feeling. She didn't care now that the man she was kissing was Giancarlo Gianni.

Chapter Ten

At first she thought it was another dream. Like the first dream it was difficult to establish where she was and she still had the sensation that she was not awake, that she was still floating above it all and that any moment she would sleep deeply and dreamlessly again. She caught glimpses of faces she recognised, Devlin and Gianni and Bruno. Why was Bruno in her dream? She didn't want to have dreams about Bruno. And where was Colette? And why was she worrying about these things if she was dreaming? It didn't matter if it was a dream.

She felt a hot pulse of sensation from her clitoris, the sensation of someone wanking her, rolling their finger over the rigid knot of flesh with perfect rhythm, the perfect amount of pressure, the sort of wanking that made her come quickly, easily. She could not see who was doing this to her and didn't care. It was a dream, another erotic dream. All she had to do was lie back and enjoy it, enjoy the feelings that her subconscious was creating for her.

It was her orgasm that woke her up. This was not the orgasm of pure sensation that she had had in her dream. This was hot and strong and real. It made her arch her back with pleasure every nerve alive. It made her want to wake up and open her eyes. But she was already awake and her eyes were already open. It was not a dream after all. It was reality, though with no sharp edges, blurred and indistinct like a picture photographed through layers of gauze.

She tried to force herself back into full consciousness but it was like trying to fight her way out of a room filled with cotton wool. She tried to move her hands but something prevented her. She twisted her head around and saw her wrists were secured above her head by padded leather cuffs attached to either side of a sturdy wooden frame. As she could not move her legs either and they were splayed apart, she imagined they were tied in a similar manner but, as yet, the edges of consciousness were still too blurred for her to see that far. The padded leather cuffs stirred a memory. She had seen them and felt them before. But where?

A wave of tiredness hit her again. She closed her eyes and for a moment almost let herself surrender to the woolly darkness that appeared so inviting. But from somewhere she found the energy to fight against it and struggled to raise her eyelids again even though they each felt weighed down by several leaden balloons. She had to keep awake and work out where she was and what was happening to her. She could hear voices now.

'She's awake.' It was Devlin. His voice sounded tense and distant.

'I want her awake.'

'See for yourself.'

Suddenly Gianni's face appeared above Stephanie. Quite extraordinarily it provoked a rush of passion in her. Her dream had been so erotic, so tangible and so totally associated in her mind with this man that she could not stop herself from being swamped with a feeling of desire for him. Her subconscious had laid out for her a perfect presentation of her sexual needs. It was a total reversal. She remembered that this had happened to her once before: a man she had strongly disliked had become an object of passion after she had experienced the female equivalent of a wet dream with the man as the main participant.

'OK,' Gianni was saying. She saw his lips move but the words seemed to come later, like a movie dubbed into a foreign language.

'So you've got what you want.'

'Yes, my friend, and in exchange I have given you what you want, so we both have satisfaction.'

'You won't regret it.'

'I know that.'

The gauze was being removed from the lens of the camera. The picture was clearing, shapes no longer merging into blocks of colour. Stephanie could distinguish edges now, though some of the corners remained indistinct. She looked around to try and see where Devlin was but she could not raise her head up off the frame by more than a few inches bound as she was. She recognised the room as part of the cellar suite, the room furnished with all the bondage equipment. She had been strapped down to one of the punishment frames about the size of a small double bed, a slatted wooden frame covered with a thin mattress. She was naked except for her sheer black stockings held up by her dark blue suspender belt. For some reason, as she could see and feel her feet now, she was still wearing her high-heeled shoes.

She felt no fear or panic. She knew she must have been drugged and brought down here. Actually she wanted to tell Gianni that as far as she was concerned her feelings for him had undergone a drastic change. She wanted him. She would only be too delighted to have him. She wanted the dream to become a reality, wanted to know whether

her subconscious was right to transpose villain to favourite. The trouble was that she couldn't seem to form any words. It was some minutes before she had worked out that she was gagged as well as bound.

'Wake up!' Gianni was saying, taking her cheeks in his hand and shaking her head. She'd thought her eyes were open. Admittedly it was not always easy to focus them. That required a little too much effort at the moment. She knew Gianni was naked because she could feel his erect penis prodding her waist as he leant over her. She felt excitement again, wanting his penis in her cunt or mouth. She remembered her distaste for him, how badly he'd behaved but now she didn't care. Now nothing mattered but her desire.

'Now I give you what you want,' Gianni said and Stephanie only wanted to say, please, please do, please give it to me now. He took her left nipple in his fingers and pinched it, then did the same with the right, then alternated between the two. Stephanie felt his penis twitch against her waist, growing harder. He ran his hand down her body until it reached her black pubic hair where it delved down to find her clitoris.

'Yes, yes,' she wanted to say.

'Such a big one,' Gianni said, tapping the knot of pink flesh with his finger.

Then he slipped his finger down between her open legs to push up between her labia. But his fingers met resistance. Stephanie was dry. She could not imagine why. She wanted him totally. She *felt* wet, she wanted to be wet. She wanted to make it easy for him to slide that wonderful cock deep into her as he had already done in her imagination. Instead she was dry. Rationally she knew it was probably a side effect of the drug. She was sure if he just rubbed her clitoris for a little longer her cunt would soon reward his persistence.

But Gianni was in no mood to be patient. Stephanie's dryness was another slap in the face of his masculinity. He was furious.

'What's the matter with you? You not like men?'

He got up on to the wooden frame and lay on top of her, pushing his penis between her labia where his fingers had been. He caught one of her breasts in his hand and squeezed it then pushed forward again with his cock. Still her body refused to lubricate.

'OK. I give you what you like. I know how you get hot.'

He climbed off the frame. After a moment he was holding something in front of Stephanie's face but not long enough for her to get her eyes to focus on it.

'See this? This is what you like.'

She wanted to tell him to work on her, to make her wet, that her body was betraying her because of the drug. She managed to produce a moan through the gag and struggle a little up towards him, but he misinterpreted her message.

'You don't get away from this,' he said.

'Let me wank her again.' It was a female voice. Stephanie recognised it but could not think who it belonged to. She looked around the room as far as she was able but could not see anyone else but Bruno standing by the wall his arms folded over his chest, and Devlin standing by her feet.

'It didn't work last time.'

That was true, Stephanie thought. How could she be so dry after that delicious orgasm? Her body was concealing her emotions though, she thought, somewhere in the back of her mind, it served them right for drugging her.

'Not that whip. It'll cut her,' the female voice was saying pointedly.

That was enough to get Stephanie to focus on the object in Gianni's hand. It was a riding crop but not with the usual thick leather loop on the tip. This crop had a thin woven tassel obviously intended to cut rather than merely slap.

'Get out,' Gianni snarled at the hidden woman.

'I'll get her wet this time,' the voice pleaded.

'I do what I want,' Gianni insisted.

Gianni swung the whip and a hot line of pain shot across the top of Stephanie's thigh. The injection of adrenaline that followed instantaneously cleared the remnants of the drug from her system. She saw Gianni's hand rise to deliver the second blow and struggled to free herself as the whip flew through the air and down on to her breasts, barely missing her nipples.

'I give what she deserves,' Gianni grunted as he aimed the third blow. Stephanie could see him clearly now, his erect penis swaying with the movement of his body, sweat already breaking out on his forehead. She could see Devlin too, at the end of the room, not able to watch what was happening. The third stroke landed in the same place as the first and this time the pain made Stephanie scream into the gag. Only a muffled moan came out. She writhed against the leather straps but they held firm.

Gianni was standing by her head now. Stephanie could see his naked buttocks as he raised the whip again, this time aiming it downward to hit the delicate folds of flesh between her open legs.

'No,' the woman's voice shouted. She leapt forward and caught Gianni's arm wrestling the whip from his grasp. 'You can't whip a woman there.'

'Give me the whip. I do what I want.'

He tried to pull the whip out of her hand but she held it firm. With her free hand she slapped Gianni's face so hard the blow knocked Gianni to his knees. Before he could recover she slapped him back-handed on the other cheek. The smack echoed through the room.

'You bitch,' Gianni snarled, getting to his feet. He

snatched for the whip again but the woman backed away. She had stepped into Stephanie's line of vision now and she saw immediately why she had recognised the voice. It was Venetia. She stood defiantly in front of Gianni, dressed in high-heeled black boots and a black Lycra catsuit that clung to every curve of her body.

'Give it to him, Venetia,' Devlin ordered, his voice hard and angry.

But before she could refuse Bruno stepped forward and pulled the whip from her hand, giving it back to Gianni. Then he caught Venetia around the waist and held her firm in a vicelike grip. Gianni raised the whip again and aimed. It hit Stephanie a glancing blow, missing her clitoris and labia and hitting the soft flesh at the top of her inner thigh. The pain was intense.

Gianni's penis was thick and harder than it had ever been.

'You want more?' he said, staring down into Stephanie's face. She shook her head as best she could, trying to make him understand with her eyes what she could not tell him with her lips. She hoped her cunt would tell him, hoped it was wet and pliant at last. She did not want another blow from the cruel whip while she lay there unable to protect herself or do anything but watch the whip fall.

Gianni thrust a finger into her. She was wet. He was not interested in finesse now. He stuck another finger alongside the first, and then a third. The penetration made her shudder. Her cunt swallowed the fingers hungrily, coating them with her juices.

'That's better,' Gianni said.

That's better, Stephanie thought.

The whipmarks on her body were throbbing and hot, as if they were on fire, especially the one on her inner thigh, not an inch away from her open cunt. But they were not throbbing with pain. It was a different sensation. The heat they produced was like the most urgent itch needing desperately to be scratched, scratched by sex, by Gianni's cock thrusting into her cunt. Only that would quench their fire.

Stephanie arched her whole body off the frame to try to tell Gianni of her need, using it to beg him to take her.

'Please, please, please,' she wanted to say.

Her cunt had never felt more in need. Her mouth felt slack, her breathing slow and heavy. The gag wasn't helping either; it reminded her too much of a cock thrust between her cheeks. She sucked on it as though it were a cock and that made her need still greater.

Gianni was smiling. He understood. Her body had delivered the message at last. He saw the desire in her eyes. It was a message he easily understood.

'I make you wait now,' he said looking into her eyes. 'You made me wait. I make you wait.'

He circled his cock with his fingers and pointed it at her face, wanking it slowly.

'Perhaps I wank on your face instead,' he teased.

Stephanie screamed into the gag what was meant to be 'No!' Only a dull moan escaped. Stephanie needed that hot spunk inside her, the way it had been inside her in the dream. The idea of it going to waste was more than she could stand. She squirmed against her bonds, trying to be seductive, trying to make him see what he would be missing.

He looked down at her superb body stretched out on the frame, the black stockings pulling at the taut blue tongues of the suspender belt, serving to emphasise the creaminess of her thighs and the openness of her cunt, her firm breasts quivering with her movement, the nipples rigid like ripe cherries and almost as red. While he still wanked his cock with one hand, he used the other to touch the red weals raised by the whip on her breasts and thigh.

Stephanie moaned from behind the gag. The weals were hot, long red streaks of sensitivity. His cool hand provoked them, renewing their effect on her, stoking their fires, making her try again to use body language to communicate her desperate need.

Gianni knew what he was doing. He ran his hand down to the weal between her thighs, the most sensitive mark of all. It felt to Stephanie as though she suddenly had another clitoris as all the nerves in the weal responded to his touch.

'You bastard,' she would have screamed. 'Fuck me, don't torture me.'

But all she could do was beg with her body and her eyes.

Almost unconsciously she was thrusting herself rhythmically off the wooden frame, undulating her buttocks and thighs. Gianni grinned broadly. He climbed on to the frame and knelt, not between her legs but over her chest, her nipples digging into the bottom of his thighs.

'I wank for you,' he said.

His hand started to move faster down his shaft. Stephanie could see a little tear of moisture develop as it worked on the hard inflamed flesh. She tried to buck him off her, she tried to plead with him with her eyes. She felt as though her cunt was so wet her juices were running out of her and down between her buttocks. She swore she had never wanted a man more and this bastard was going to make her watch him wank.

But Gianni had other ideas.

'Take her gag out,' he said to Venetia. Bruno released her immediately and she came to stand behind Stephanie's head, unstrapping the leather gag and pulling it clear of her mouth. Before Stephanie could utter a word Gianni had leant forward and pushed his cock between her lips. His penis felt hot in her mouth. Gianni grabbed Venetia's hand and pulled her towards him.

'You're going to help me,' he said.

He moved to kiss her on the mouth but she turned her head away. He made a grab for one of her large breasts through the clinging Lycra but she caught his hand before it reached its target.

'Not me,' Venetia said angrily, shaking free from his grasp.

His anger returned. He pulled out of Stephanie's mouth. He glared at Devlin, his eyes full of reproach. For a moment he rested on his haunches looking down at Stephanie's face. It was as though he was deciding what to do, punish Venetia or fuck Stephanie. Then he made his decision. He eased himself down Stephanie's body until he was positioned with his cock so close to her labia she could feel its heat. He did nothing then, looking straight into her eyes.

'You want?'

'Yes, oh yes.' Her voice sounded strange to her, at least an octave lower than normal.

'You want?' he repeated.

'Yes,' she screamed. 'Yes, yes, yes!'

He plunged his cock forward, ramming it into her body. Stephanie almost came on his first stroke as she felt what she had craved for so long slide up her soaking wet cunt, right up till she could feel his balls knocking against her arse. He pulled back and bucked forward again and again and again. Each stroke seemed to be harder and stronger, pushing farther and farther into her, laying her open, splitting her. There was nothing she could do to stop herself from toppling into orgasm, feeling sensations from her clitoris and nipples that were familiar, and new sensations from the red weals he had inflicted on her body throbbing with the same intensity as her cunt, reflecting and amplifying her pleasure. She could hear herself screaming 'yes, yes, yes' she could hear herself moaning. He was coming too. She could feel his penis swell inside her, feel her cunt.

squeezing on it involuntarily as his spunk jetted into her. She could not tell whether this had brought her off again or whether his spunking at that moment had merely intensified the orgasm she was already having. It didn't matter. Only the feeling mattered.

As she felt his body relax, all the thrusting gone, her natural instinct was to wrap her arms around his back. But in the heat of her passion she had forgotten her bonds. The sudden jolt of restraint as she tried to move sent another shudder of pleasure through her body, like an aftershock of an earthquake. Deliberately she flexed her ankles against the cuffs, trying to close her legs, wanting the feeling of restraint to provoke another wave of emotion. It made her feel helpless, open, available. It made her feel she had been used. It brought back memories of the intense excitement she had felt the first time she had experienced bondage. It made her feel unbelievably wanton, her open cunt the centre of her being. And despite what had just happened it made her feel incredibly turned on. She wanted more.

Gianni did not wait for his cock to shrink. He pulled out of Stephanie and stood up, his cock glistening with her juices and, no doubt, some of his own. As her view was no longer obstructed by Gianni's body Stephanie could see Devlin again, standing by her feet. He had stripped off his tie and the jacket of his suit, and undone the top button of his shirt. He was looking at her, staring at the long slit of her sex, her pubic hair matted and wet, a dribble of Gianni's spunk already running out of her. She recognised the look in his eyes; she had seen it before during this weekend. It was a look of unabated lust. Quite deliberately she pushed her cunt up off the frame towards him, as much as the bonds would allow, taunting him with it.

He came up to her and touched the side of her cheek with his hand.

'I'm sorry,' he whispered, not wanting Gianni to hear. 'It was the only way. I had to do it.'

She looked into his eyes but said nothing. She was furious with him rationally and in due course she would make him pay for what he had done to her. But, at the moment, it was other feelings, the feelings in every nerve in her body, that dominated her consciousness. Her sexuality was too strong, too aroused to stop for rational analysis now. That would come later, much later.

Gianni had slipped into one of the ubiquitous towelling robes provided by Bruno. He pointed at Venetia. Devlin knew what was coming next.

'I want her punished, Devlin. You see what she did?'

'Yes.' Devlin sighed. He'd hoped Gianni would be satisfied and go. He turned to Venetia. 'That was a very silly thing to do. You shouldn't have interfered,' he said quietly.

'I want to see her punished.'

'Couldn't we . . .?'

'No. She's one of your whores, isn't she?'

'He was going to whip her cunt, Devlin,' Venetia spat the words out. 'You can't do that to a woman. Not with that whip.'

'I thought we had, what you say, a deal?' Gianni said.

'She was trying to help me, Devlin,' Stephanie added.

'Don't interfere. You don't understand. Venetia's a slave like all the others, a thief. I have to punish her.' He whispered this into Stephanie's ear while he stroked her cheek tenderly.

'Untie me, Devlin,' Stephanie said forcefully.

'Not if you're going to interfere.'

'I won't,' she said and meant it.

Devlin nodded to Bruno who quickly unbuckled the straps at Stephanie's wrists and ankles. She sat up on the frame massaging the circulation back into her limbs.

'I thought we had an agreement, Venetia,' Devlin was saying. 'I thought we had an understanding. Haven't I always kept my part of the bargain? Haven't I? I've never asked you to do anything you haven't wanted to do, have I?'

'No, but . . .'

'I've always respected your preferences, haven't I?'

'Yes,' Venetia said quietly.

'And then when it's most important, the *most* important, you let me down.' Devlin sat down on the wooden frame next to Stephanie. 'You see, my dear, Venetia likes only women. When she first came here she begged me not to make her have men. And since she begged so prettily and I am naturally a soft understanding person and had quite a few women associates with the same preferences, I saw no reason not to accommodate her. A bargain I have always kept until now.'

Bruno grabbed Venetia from behind, his arms circling her waist and enclosing hers. Venetia made no attempt to struggle. He clipped one cuff of a pair of handcuffs on to her left wrist, then twisted the right behind her back to be manacled together. He had clipped them tight, and the cold metal was biting into her flesh.

'Don't hurt her, Devlin,' Stephanie whispered.

'I have to,' Devlin replied.

A strange sensation swept over Stephanie as he said it. Suddenly she knew she wanted to see what was going to happen to Venetia. She wanted it because she knew it would turn her on, knew it would feed the fire of sexuality that burnt in her body. She was so turned on, so hot, she thought almost anything would serve to increase her heat and pleasure. Her mind was full of images and feelings. She thought of herself spreadeagled under Gianni, his cock poised above her as he teased her, making her beg to be taken, and could not suppress a shudder of pleasure.

'What are you going to do?' she asked trying to keep the excitement out of her voice. Devlin had given Bruno his instructions.

'You know, don't you, Venetia?'

'Don't. Please,' Venetia said, knowing he would not be swayed.

'This I like to see.' Gianni said from where he sat in a high-backed chair usually used for bondage, sipping a brandy provided by Bruno.

Stephanie could see the edge of excitement in his eyes. Whatever Devlin wanted from him she was sure, after tonight, and promises of other nights, it would be delivered. He had the air of a man who was discovering pleasures he had never dreamt of, pleasures he intended to repeat. The castle was the bait. However the fish was hooked, however it squirmed on the line, as Gianni had done, once it had taken the bait it would never escape. It would want more and more of what only Devlin and the castle could provide. Gianni was ensnared now, there was no question of that.

And in a different way Devlin and the castle had ensnared Stephanie too. There was no doubt as to what she was feeling now. Her body quivering with excitement, stretched taut with sexual tension as surely as if she had still been tied to the frame. Despite the fact Venetia was going to be punished for trying to help her, Stephanie wanted to see what was going to happen next, wanted to be part of it. Perhaps she would have felt differently had Devlin not told her Venetia was, in fact, a slave. Perhaps.

'Please, Devlin . . .'

But Devlin nodded to Bruno who immediately left the room to follow Devlin's whispered instructions. Venetia stood tall in the black catsuit, her hands manacled behind her back, her full breasts thrust out. For a moment there was silence, the room still. A sense of expectancy hung heavily in the air.

The price of Gianni's cooperation was high. He had demanded Stephanie, a woman who had given Devlin unprecedented sexual spontaneity. After the failed attempt to distract him with Colette Gianni had been so angry that he had threatened to leave the island, taking the unsigned contract and Devlin's future with him. Fortunately, his infatuation with Stephanie was so complete, despite its suddenness, that when Devlin suggested an alternative means of achieving his ends he had suspended his usual need for conquest and had been tempted down to the cellars. And now Venetia, the only woman he had caught whom he had ever really cared for and come to trust, had to be sacrificed as well. He did not blame her for trying to protect Stephanie. He knew Stephanie had a way of provoking an unusually strong sexual response and in London, Venetia had told him, this is precisely what she had experienced. Her experience with Stephanie had affected her deeply; she had never had such feelings with a woman. But what Gianni wanted, Gianni got. There was no other way of dealing with the situation until the contract was signed. Then, and only then, the deal would be done. He would never allow himself to get into this financial position again. He had too much to risk. He had been taught a lesson he intended never to forget.

The heavy wooden door swung open and Bruno entered, leading the masked man into the room rather as he would a dog, by a chain attached to a studded leather collar around the slave's neck. He was no longer wearing the bright carnival mask Stephanie had seen this morning and on the plane; Bruno had replaced it with a hood made of tight black elasticated material which covered the whole head apart from the eyes. There was no opening for his mouth and, presumably, as he had been on the plane, he was effectively gagged. Whoever the man was his desire to remain anonymous was being well respected – Bruno was certainly in no position to spill the beans. And no one here would recognise him in this hood. On his left ankle he still wore the metal cuff that had been used to chain him to the floor of the cell. As with all the male slaves, he wore a hard leather pouch chained over his genitals.

Bruno unclipped the chain from the leather collar. The eyes staring out from the black mask were fixed on the near-naked Stephanie. They were more in evidence than they had been behind the carnival mask on the plane. They were the very grey blue eyes, she thought, of a man older than his body would suggest. He stood upright, his body firm and muscled. Obviously this was a man who looked after himself and exercised regularly. Stephanie noticed that the black pubic hair escaping from under the leather pouch was dotted with grey hairs. It ran up to his navel in ragged clumps before it petered out. His chest was hairy too but again only in clumps, it was not like the carpet of hair Devlin had. This hair too was beginning to grey.

'Can we get on with it?' Gianni said irritably. He leant forward in his chair.

'Bruno,' Devlin said, indicating Venetia.

Bruno stepped forward and caught Venetia by the upper arm. His other hand ran down the front of the shiny Lycra catsuit and grabbed the material that covered her crotch. He held her by this, released her arm and fumbled in his black tunic with his free hand, coming out with a wicked-looking hunting knife. Venetia immediately started to struggle, trying to free herself from Bruno's grip.

'Devlin,' Stephanie said quietly, clutching Devlin's arm in panic.

'Don't worry,' he said. 'He's not going to hurt you, Venetia. Keep still.'

Venetia obeyed but kept her eyes on the knife.

Bruno pulled on the material, pulling it as far away from

145

her body as the tightness of the Lycra would allow. Then he simply sliced around the cloth he had gathered in his hand with the razor-sharp blade of the knife. The Lycra sprung back into place, leaving Bruno with the handful he had sawn away, and Venetia's body exposed from the top of her pubic triangle to the cleft of her arse. Using the same technique Bruno pulled on the material covering each of her large breasts until each in turn was exposed by ragged holes in the black Lycra.

'Bellissima!' Gianni cried, applauding Bruno's invention.

Unable to ripen fully, the masked man's erection strained against the hard pouch. His eyes were on Venetia now that her body was exposed, gazing on her thick heavy breasts in such contrast to her slim waist and slender hips. The wisps of her meagre pubic hair barely covered the joining of her labia. She was a stunningly beautiful creature and it was obvious to the man what he had been brought here to do. As if to confirm it, Bruno had sheathed the knife and was unlocking the small padlock that held the genital pouch in place. As it fell away the masked man's erection sprung free.

'No, Devlin,' Venetia begged quietly, as though trying not to let anyone else in the room hear. 'Please, Devlin. You know I've never had a man, please ...'

'She's a virgin!' Gianni had heard her perfectly. 'Well, now, this is better and better.'

His greedy eyes looked at Venetia with renewed interest. The masked man had heard too. With the incident on the plane and now this, Devlin was certainly orchestrating a weekend for him that he would never forget.

'Devlin ...' Venetia begged again, looking straight into Devlin's eyes. For a moment Stephanie could see he was tempted to let her off. But he had no choice. Gianni was paying the piper.

'Get on with it,' he said with no conviction.

Bruno took the masked man by the arm and led him towards Venetia. She made no attempt to move. The masked man looked back at Devlin as if for reassurance that this wasn't some elaborate game and that he had misunderstood his role. He had visited the castle many times and knew there were many games and many rules and that the price for breaking the rules was paid in pain. Caught in a trough of indecision, his feelings for Venetia weighing heavily on him as she continued to beg with her eyes not to commission this act, Devlin did nothing.

'Tomorrow is the sixteenth, my friend. You need me to remind you of this? The day your loan runs out.' Gianni's voice was ice cold. His eyes did not leave the glories of Venetia's body as he spoke. He would get what he wanted. Power over a man of Devlin's wealth was a rare commodity and he was determined to use it while he could. Tomorrow, with the contract signed, Devlin would not be so malleable.

'What are you waiting for?' Devlin growled at the masked man.

He needed no second bidding. The man's erection and his balls ached for relief. He pulled back his foreskin over the head of his penis and felt an instant jolt of pleasure. It was the first time he'd been able to touch himself since he was put on the plane. A tear of fluid had already formed in his excitement. He was three or four feet in front of Venetia. She had given up the attempt to influence Devlin and now her bright green eyes were watching him closely. The man edged forward and she backed away. There wasn't far for her to go. In two steps her manacled hands were pressed into the stone wall of the cellar.

The masked man advanced slowly. Venetia moved sideways, away into the farthest corner of the room. The man followed, his erection bobbing out in front of him. She reached the corner and pressed herself into it. He stood in front of her. Their eyes met. Hunter and prey. Venetia tensed her body. With her hands cuffed behind her back there was little she could do to defend herself but she was going to make it as difficult for him as she could.

The man lunged forward but Venetia was ready for him. As he tried to grab her shoulders she ducked down and pushed passed him knocking him off balance as her shoulders slammed into his hip. He sprawled on to the cold stone floor, only just managing to break his fall with his hands.

Gianni was laughing and applauding. '*Bellissima bella*,' he cried reminding Stephanie of a man applauding the first pass of a matador.

Venetia was in the middle of the room now, able to dart in any direction to escape her pursuer. Only the various items of bondage apparatus, the chairs, whipping stools, and punishment frames, were in her way. The masked man had picked himself up from the floor and advanced towards her again, angry at her now. But Venetia made sure she did not get herself cornered and always circled to the centre of the room. The cat-and-mouse game continued for some minutes, with neither the masked man's appetite nor his erection in the least diminished by the game.

Gianni watched fascinated, his eyes constantly roving over Venetia's body so wantonly displayed by the holes cut in the black Lycra and accentuated by the sharp high heels of her boots. But Devlin wanted it over.

'Bruno . . .'

Bruno was standing behind Venetia. Before she could react to the new threat he had jumped forward and caught her around her waist.

'No, not fair,' Gianni shouted in mock complaint. But he did not want Bruno actually to release her.

The masked man stood in front of Venetia and took one of her large breasts in his hand. Venetia struggled against

Bruno's grip but it was as though his arms were made of steel. The hand squeezed and pummelled at the soft flesh of her tit, then the fingers took the nipple and squeezed and pinched this too. The masked man repeated the process with the other breast, all the time looking straight into Venetia's green eyes to see her response, the tip of his penis nudging the wispy hair of her pubis. Venetia's nipples were hard now, her body betraying her, though her eyes betrayed nothing.

His hand pried between her legs. She clasped them together tightly but not enough to prevent his forefinger finding the tight node of her clitoris. As she felt him manipulate it she renewed her struggle against Bruno but this only provoked him to hold her around the neck and clamp his hand on her chin, making it impossible for her to move her head. The finger pried deeper, despite the resistance of her thighs, and wanked her clitoris. Against her will Venetia could sense some wetness beginning to lubricate her labia. The masked man felt it too.

As if she weighed nothing, Bruno picked her bodily off the floor. The masked man's finger never lost contact with her clitoris for a second, clamped there as it was by her thighs, as Bruno laid Venetia down on one of the wooden frames. As she felt the rough material of the thin mattress that covered the frame on her back Venetia realised the inevitable. Resistance was impossible. With her hands still manacled behind her back her weight rested on them forcing her to arch her back, angling her cunt up as if in invitation.

She felt the masked man's hand pushing her legs apart. She did not resist. She did not cooperate either. She lay passive and hoped it would be over quickly. She tried to imagine she was somewhere else. She cursed herself for ever getting into this position, for stealing from Devlin and for imagining he would not, sooner or later, exact this punishment on her. She had been his special slave. Now her luck had run out.

Bruno knelt by the frame, his hand gripping her throat. The masked man pressed two fingers into her cunt, feeling the soft wet walls of it, pushing as far as his fingers would go then pulling out again, imitating the movement his cock would make very soon now.

Venetia strained her head to look around the room. Gianni sat on the edge of his chair his eyes fixed on her body. Stephanie sat watching too. Only Devlin appeared not to be able to bring himself to look.

'Fuck her then,' Gianni prompted. She could see his robe had fallen open and he was stroking his own semierect cock.

The masked man needed no further encouragement. He climbed on to her body and felt her shudder as his cock lay on her navel. He half expected her to start to fight again, to try to buck and twist him off her. But she lay still, seemingly accepting the inevitable. Slowly he raised his buttocks and aimed his cock down between her legs. He could feel the soft flesh of her labia on his cock already wet from his own excretions. He pushed it down farther until it was at the entrance to her cunt. He looked down at her magnificent body, the black Lycra clinging to every inch of her that was not already white and exposed. Then in one smooth movement he buried his cock up to the hilt in her wet cunt knowing he was the first man who had ever penetrated her.

Venetia screamed once, a long thin piercing scream. She tried to take her mind away, tried to think of other things, of being in another place, tried to pretend she could not feel this man inside her body, fucking her, but it was impossible. He was thrusting in and out, the relentless rhythm of his cock and the constant hammering of her clitoris against his pubic bone making it impossible for her to be anywhere but in that room feeling what he was doing to her and knowing what was coming, that for the first time a man was going to spunk inside her. She was fighting herself too she began to realise. Almost involuntarily she tried to squirm away from the cock that was giving her a feeling she didn't want, a feeling of pleasure. But the rhythm was irresistible, unyielding. She did not know whether the masked man was a good lover, she had nothing to compare him with, but his thrusts seemed never ending and the force and power of his cock overwhelmed her.

Her tits ached from the treatment he had given them, but it was not real pain. Her cunt was stretched by the sword of flesh ramming into it. It was not like a dildo, not like the dildos she had used and had been used on her, cold and dead. His cock was hot and alive, swelling with its load of spunk.

She fought the pleasure, determined she would not let it take her over. Her body was betraying her again. Then Bruno was gone and Stephanie knelt in his place. Instead of his iron hand holding her throat Stephanie was stroking her face, her neck, even her eyelids. Stephanie was there as the cock relentlessly forced her to orgasm. It was Stephanie's hand stretching down her body, running her fingers down her open thigh, so tender, that brought her off, opened the nerves of her body. It was Stephanie's kiss and Stephanie's tongue in her mouth as though wanting to touch her orgasm and be part of it that made Venetia feel she would never stop coming, made her whole body quiver and shake under and over and around a man for the first time in her life.

The masked man had managed not to spunk. He waited. He waited as he watched Stephanie walking towards the frame, watched her stroke her friend and kiss her friend. He waited as he felt Venetia's orgasm rake through every nerve in her long beautiful body. Then he knew it was his turn. As Venetia subsided beneath him he knew it was his turn. He looked at Stephanie, remembering what she had done to him on the plane, as she got to her feet, naked but for her tautly suspended stockings and high heels. He knew what she was going to do before she did it. He even knew why – because she wanted him finished with her friend. Then her hand was down between his legs to where he was coupled to Venetia, down in all the heat and wetness, down cupping his balls, pulling them away from his body, squeezing them with just the right amount of pressure, making sure his spunk was in his cock. Her fingers wrapped themselves around his cock now on his outward stroke and tightened around it and that was the last thing he felt before he surrendered himself to his climax, before he bucked into Venetia and spunked, spunked so hard and so long his body seemed out of his control for what seemed like forever, wanting only to get the last drop of spunk out and into her.

Stephanie had been unable to sit and watch passively. She had seen the change in Venetia; she had watched the tense resistance of her body, fighting every touch, change to passivity, then relax slowly and change again, as passivity had given way to desire, as Venetia's body had started to crave and want what the masked man was giving her. Only with her eyes did Venetia express her true feelings. Stephanie had wanted to watch what was going to happen to Venetia. The idea had turned her on, had increased the sexual arousal she was already experiencing, twisting another notch higher on the rachet of her desire.

At first she had stood up only to get a better view as Venetia was laid on the frame. She had done it unconsciously, enthralled by the spectacle before her eyes. In the same way she had moved closer, only dimly aware of Gianni's eyes on her near-naked body. She had watched as the masked man thrust his cock into Venetia and heard

Venetia's heart-rent scream. But Stephanie was not content to watch, her body and her temperament needed something more. Without asking Devlin, or Gianni – the ring-master of this particular circus – for that matter, she knelt besides Bruno and pulled his hand from Venetia's throat. Bruno acquiesced after a nod of approval from Devlin. He got to his feet and walked away. Stephanie caressed Venetia's throat where the strong fingers had left an impression on her white skin, and their eyes met. She felt the sexual electricity that Venetia's body was generating; she stroked her body, her neck, her face, her thighs, then kissed Venetia's mouth. As her tongue penetrated her mouth she felt the orgasm rocking through Venetia's body, and knew she, and not the man, had given her that release. She could see it in Venetia's eyes, her gratitude and a plea. She knew immediately what Venetia wanted. Venetia wanted this man out of her, wanted it to be over.

And Stephanie knew what to do. She had become expert now. She knew she could milk this man, take his balls in her hand and milk the spunk out of him. She knew she could make him come instantly and Venetia's punishment would be over and Gianni satisfied. She had felt down between his legs, felt his balls wet with Venetia's juices. She squeezed them, pulled them, felt his cock swell with spunk. She circled his cock with her fingers putting greater pressure on it than Venetia's cunt could do. And that had taken him over the edge, made him shoot his spunk, unable to hold back any longer. Stephanie had made him come too.

'Bravo! Bravo!' Gianni was shouting, Caesar satisfied with the fate of the gladiators, both thumbs turned up.

The masked man was led away, Bruno attaching the chain to his leather collar and taking him out of the room, his cock still half erect and wet. Stephanie had found the key to the handcuffs and made Venetia roll on to her side so that she could free her from the steel hoops. When they were off she helped her massage the deep red marks on her wrists where the metal had bitten into her flesh as they were forced to bear the weight of two bodies.

'Go and get some rest now,' Stephanie said.

'I'll be all right.' Venetia touched her hand to Stephanie's cheek. 'Thank you,' she added.

'Go.' Stephanie insisted. 'We'll talk tomorrow.'

No one interfered as Venetia got unsteadily to her feet and walked out of the room.

Stephanie's concern for her friend was fleeting, her concern for herself was taking precedence over everything. It was becoming overwhelming. What she had just done and felt had further cranked up her sexual arousal. Her whole body seemed to be alive; the red weals from the whip were throbbing with a sexual pulse that was spreading through her. It was as though her body had turned into one huge erogenous zone. Venetia's touch, gentle and soft, was transposed by Stephanie's fevered body into the most intimate of caresses.

It was not only her body, Stephanie knew. It was what was going on in her mind. She was in control again. She had enjoyed the sensation of submission but in the end it was control that was her turn-on. That was what she had discovered last night with Devlin and this morning with the slaves. It was not something she would have expected of herself but it was something she was perfectly happy to exploit. As she stood in this strange room surrounded by sexual paraphernalia of every sort, she knew she was in charge. She had become the ring-master, she was in command. And it was this that thrilled her and gave an extra dimension to her sexual awareness.

She walked towards Gianni, slowly and deliberately looking steadily into his eyes, demanding that his gaze did not drift down, as she knew he wanted it to, to take in the sensuous movement of her stockinged legs as nylon rasped against nylon and the dark hairy pubic triangle. She dared him to look down, dared him to disobey her. Gianni was in her thrall.

Pulling him to his feet she kissed him hard on the mouth pushing her tongue between his lips and allowing him to do the same with her. She ran her fingers under the towelling robe until she could reach his back, then she gouged it viciously from top to bottom with her long fingernails. He winced.

'Delicate little thing, aren't we?' she mocked. 'You're going to fuck me again, Gianni. And this time I won't be tied down.' She wanted his cock inside her. But that was not all she wanted. She turned to Devlin. 'And so are you.'

She turned on her heels and walked out of the stone-walled punishment room, her words still hanging in the air. For a moment her anger at the way Devlin had treated her, at what he had done and allowed to be done to her and to Venetia, was pushed to the back of her mind. She would make him pay for that undoubtedly, but now other priorities took precedence over revenge.

She walked down the soft-carpeted corridor of the cellar suite where she had been this morning and where, presumably, Bruno had carried her, drugged and unconscious, some hours before. She found her way to the bathroom, turned on the shower to full power, stripped off her stockings and suspender belt and stood in the invigorating cascade of water. She towelled herself dry and wandered into one of the bedrooms of the suite. The one she chose was decorated in blue tones, silk pastel blue wall-coverings and a dark blue carpet similar to the one in her bedroom upstairs. She pulled the toning blue counterpane off the bed and lay on the cool silk sheet underneath. For a while she did nothing, enjoying the comfort and softness of the bed after the hardness and discomfort of the wooden punishment frame. Then she opened her legs, spreading them wide apart, bending her knees so she could see the smooth curves of the muscles in her thighs. Her long lithe legs were definitely her best feature. She looked down at her body, at her breasts, flattened slightly by gravity, her tight corrugated nipples, her dark pubic hair newly fluffed up by the towel, and was pleased at what she saw.

Looking sheepish, Gianni came in first his arrogant manner for some reason evaporated. Now he looked like a junior clerk summoned to the manager's office for the first time and expecting the worst.

'You're very lovely,' he said tentatively, unable to take his eyes off Stephanie's naked body. Her legs were still open and one hand casually stroked her pubic hair rather as one might stroke a cat. This cat was anxious to be fed.

'Where's Devlin?' Stephanie asked sharply. Devlin came into the room and closed the door behind him. He had changed from shirt and trousers and was now wearing a white towelling robe identical to the one Gianni was wearing except that Devlin's was monogrammed on the pocket with the letter D in gold stitching. Unlike Gianni, Devlin did not look at all intimidated.

'This is what you want is it? The two of us?' he said, in a voice that was harsh and stern.

'Yes,' she replied trying to judge his mood. She was not going to let him take the initiative. 'This is exactly what I want. It's time for what I want, isn't it?'

Devlin was about to say something but stopped himself.

'She is so beautiful, yes?' Gianni said.

'She is more than beautiful. And she knows it,' Devlin commented.

'What are you waiting for?' Stephanie prompted, the animal she was stroking between her legs getting increasingly impatient.

Devlin sat on the bed by Stephanie's foot and bent to kiss her ankle. It was a gesture of acquiescence. He knew it and so did Stephanie. She would get her way. The kiss turned to a sort of playful bite, then back to a kiss again as his mouth moved up along the arch of her foot and he started to suck her toes.

'Do the other one then. Don't just stand there,' she barked at Gianni who immediately did as he was told, starting with the ankle just as Devlin had done before working along the foot to suck each toe in turn. Both men could not resist looking up the long legs to where the lips of Stephanie's cunt nestled in the thick forest of curly pubic hair. Her hand was still stroking the hair and as they watched she moved her finger down to her clitoris to stroke that too.

Gianni stripped off his robe. Devlin did the same. The pattern was set now. Devlin moved up her left leg, trailing his lips along her flesh, sometimes trailing his tongue too, sometimes stopping to kiss or nibble at a particular place, the middle of her calf, her knee, a piece of outer thigh. And taking his lead from Devlin, Gianni followed suit. Whatever Devlin did, he did. Their hands caressed her too, four hands moulding, smoothing, pawing her long legs. Stephanie closed her eyes and abandoned herself to the excess of sensation.

Devlin's mouth reached the top of the strong curve of her thigh and began to desend into the valley of her cunt.

'Not yet,' Stephanie said petulantly, slapping Devlin lightly on the cheek.

So he began to move his mouth up her body along her left side as Gianni followed on the right. They moved from her side to her navel and then back again, covering every inch of her flesh with their mouths, with their little kisses, their hot tongues, and their four eager hands.

Stephanie had never experienced this before. The sensation was incredible. It was like being eaten alive. Every nerve of her body being forced to react sexually, to feel the sexual impulse usually reserved for the organs of sex. Her cunt was throbbing, the animal between her legs content for the moment to be petted and wait until it was time to be fed.

Devlin's mouth had reached her breast now. He was subtle. He didn't immediately lunge for her nipple. He used his mouth to go all around her breasts, the swell of flesh above her nipple, the crease of flesh to the side and underneath where the weight of the breast lay, using his tongue to probe into the creases as though they were little cunts. Gianni did the same, their heads only a foot apart. Stephanie waited, knowing the thrill she would get when both her nipples were sucked at the same time.

She was not disappointed. Devlin's mouth finally centred on the hard dark red bud of flesh, flicking it with his tongue first, teasing it back and forth. Gianni was less subtle this time. He sucked the nipple deep into his mouth clamping it between his teeth immediately, letting Devlin follow his lead this time, until both men's teeth were buried in the soft puckered flesh, biting, sucking, pulling at each nipple while their hands kneaded the breasts, feeding the flesh into their mouths.

Their hands were all over her. Fingers, palms, thumbs caressing and nipping and pawing and exploring every inch of her body, as far as they could reach without releasing the nipples from their mouths. Often the hands would bump into each other, both wanting the same piece of flesh. They wouldn't stop to argue, however. Stephanie had enough for all four hands. They would hurry on their way to find a new uncluttered area to explore. Stephanie felt her cunt invaded tentatively, the hand perhaps expecting a rebuke. When none came its touch hardened, finding her clitoris, penetrating her vagina.

Unrestricted now, the hands roamed free. Stephanie felt her clitoris wanked by one hand then by another. Her arse was invaded. She thought she could recognise the touch of Devlin's huge fingers but she was experiencing such a mélange of feelings she could not even be sure of that. She could feel their hard cocks poking into her sides as they moved over her body. Her cunt was running with juices, her mind a fever of sensation and images.

'Fuck me now,' she cried unable to resist the need they had created in her for a moment longer. In the depth of all these feelings though, she was still capable of a degree of rational thought. She knew it had to be Gianni first. If Devlin fucked her first she would never feel Gianni's cock afterwards. Devlin would open her too much for that.

'Gianni,' she said pulling him up by his arm. 'Fuck me. Gianni. I want it!'

He did not need much encouragement. She looked down to see his cock. It stood upright thrusting out from his body. He moved down between her legs. Devlin's mouth was still on her nipple, sucking and biting it in turn but he knew he had to abandon it now and leave room for Gianni to do her bidding. Gianni slid between Stephanie's open legs and used his hand to guide his cock to the entrance of her cunt. Devlin watched avidly as Gianni held his cock still for a half-second before plunging it into her waiting cunt. It was so wet that his stroke carried him all the way up, up to the hilt, his pubic bone jarring her clitoris. Stephanie almost screamed with pleasure. Devlin prevented it, however, as his mouth descended on hers, gagging her with his tongue.

Gianni was going mad. He was so turned on by this incredible woman, by this whole situation that he was out of control. He did not have the ability to use slow regular strokes, to work on her gradually, to practise his technique.

He could only fuck her furiously, plunging in and out of her, panting for breath, pouring with sweat, fucking her like an animal, faster and harder than he'd ever done in his life, nothing between him and his need to come.

Stephanie had had her first orgasm when the two men had taken her nipples in their mouths. She had had another when Gianni had first plunged into her cunt in one uninterrupted stroke. Now his hammering thrusts were giving her orgasm after orgasm, taking her out of all control of her body, giving her one continuous shattering concentration of feeling, each climax, like the waves of a violent storm at sea, breaking over her with greater and greater intensity. There was no beginning and no end, only a wave of passion carrying her higher and deeper into herself. And she wanted more.

'Bugger me, Gianni. Bugger me. I want it!' Somewhere inside all the passion the voice of logic still worked for her. She wanted to be buggered, knew that would give her more feeling. But only Gianni could do that for her. Devlin would split her in two.

Gianni slipped out of her cunt panting for breath, his cock glistening with her juices. She felt the four hands turning her over on to her stomach. Gianni probed her arse with his finger. It was tight but very wet. The juices from her cunt had run down between her legs, amply lubricating the niche of her arse. He positioned himself quickly, his excitement making him anxious to be back inside her. The way she had said it, demanded to be buggered, ran through his mind. No woman had ever asked him for it before. Stephanie cocked her arse up towards him to give him easier access, to get the angle right. She was anxious too, wanting to feel him buried in her arse, eagerly anticipating the feeling it would give her.

Gianni and Devlin exchanged a look. Did Gianni see envy in Devlin's eyes, envy of something he would never be able to do? Stephanie felt his cock at the entrance but he was hesitating and hesitation did not suit her mood.

'Give it to me!' she almost screamed, thrusting back at him, unable to take his cock into her without his pressure.

He pushed forward, taking his cock into her arse but only by an inch. Stephanie tensed, a momentary wave of panic flooding through her as hurt took her breath away and her mind told her she could not endure it. But it was gone just as suddenly as it had come and the frisson of fear served only to increase the sexual spiral.

'Do it. Do it,' she said quietly so he would know she really meant it.

And he did. He pushed the rest of his cock deep into her arse. It was not wet enough to penetrate in one stroke, as he had her cunt, but in two or three it was as liquid and his cock was fully home. She could not help but scream with the rush of pain. But Gianni was in no mood to hesitate now. He wanted to spunk. His whole body was focused on his cock and his overwhelming need to spunk hard and deep inside her hot little arse. It was tighter than her cunt and hotter. He rammed back and forth as frantically as he had in her cunt. He could not think of her now, only of himself. She had begged him for this and he was giving it to her. Her words echoed in his mind, 'Bugger me. I want it. Bugger me, Gianni.'

Any pain Stephanie had felt at the beginning was now overtaken by the pleasure. The pain was the pleasure now, indistinguishable as her orgasm started in series again, one after another ripping through her nerves, blacking out anything but the feeling of his hot cock thrusting into her arse.

She was saying something he could not understand. He was not even certain they were words at all, just sounds whimpered out as he felt her body pitching into orgasm. Her arse seemed to cling to him, as it was not as wet as her cunt, producing a suction on his cock, wanting to drain the spunk out of him. He could not hold back. He didn't want to hold back. Every stimulus his cock could want it had, touch, sight, sound and mental image. All at once. 'Bugger me, Gianni.' The words echoed in his mind as he felt his spunk shoot into her arse and he bucked his hips to get it all into her.

As he came his cock swelled. In the tight confines of her arse, less elastic than her cunt, the extra size sent Stephanie into the paroxysm of yet another climax so close on the tail of the last that it almost doubled a feeling that was already devastating.

For a moment no one moved. Then Stephanie felt Devlin's hand gently caressing her shoulder. Gianni's cock was shrinking rapidly but this time he let it slip naturally from her body. She lay on her stomach, her eyes closed, feeling Devlin's huge hand gently stroking her back with the lightest of touches. But the gentleness did not last long. Stephanie did not want it to last long either. Turning her head to one side she could see Devlin's cock inches away from her mouth, gnarled with veins, ugly but hard and hot. She was not going to finish anything until she had taken him again, experienced that mammoth cock filling every inch of her cunt. The thought alone, despite everything she had been through already, could not fail to produce a shiver of anticipation in her.

She only had to move her head slightly to capture the cock in her mouth. Devlin moaned as her lips wrapped around the sensitive skin of his glans and she sucked it into her mouth. Without taking her mouth away she got up on her knees and made Devlin lie back on the bed, his legs apart. Then she took the massive cock in both her hands and held it firm and tight while she tried to see how much of it she could take in her mouth. She relaxed her throat muscles then swallowed the cock, feeling it drive into her until it was at the back of her throat. But then this did not bring it more than halfway down the stem. She pulled it out, then used her saliva to wet it, running her tongue all over the hard flesh before pushing her mouth down on it again until his glans was buried at the back of her throat. This time she held it there, able to resist the temptation to gag, while she used one hand to wank the stem of his cock and the other to squeeze and pull at his balls. She felt his cock twitch with excitement. She knew she could make him come like this. But her cunt wanted him too. After what Gianni had done to her arse, and the feeling of his spunk in there still, her cunt was feeling neglected. It wanted spunk too.

Stephanie pulled her mouth off his cock. She swung her leg over his body and raised herself on her haunches reaching back behind her buttocks to guide his cock to the entrance of her cunt with her hand. His cock seemed to be throbbing in her fingers, hot and anxious for its fulfilment. She could feel her juices run from her body annointing the helmet of his cock as she placed it between the labia.

'Do you want to fuck me, Devlin?' she taunted him, pulling her cunt away from his cock for a moment.

'You know I do.'

'You don't deserve to fuck me, do you?'

'No,' he said, looking straight into her eyes, hoping against hope that this was a game and that she had no intention of really denying him.

For a long time – it was only seconds but to Devlin it felt like hours – Stephanie did nothing, enjoying the sensation of teasing him. She eased herself back until his cock was touching her labia again. She watched Devlin's expression change from anticipation that she was going to give him what he craved, to fear that she was not, as she did not make any attempt to push down further.

'You'll get what you deserve tomorrow,' she said and impaled herself on his cock letting all her weight fall on it, skewering herself down until it would go no further. The feeling took her breath away. Every inch of her cunt was full and stretched to its limit. Her mind emptied of thoughts of revenge, of everything and anything but the cock that was filling her. Her whole body began to tremble as slowly she lifted herself off his cock and drew it out only to impale herself again, driving it back in as far as she dared.

Devlin pulled her down from her squatting position so he could kiss her on the mouth. Her breasts pressed into the wiry hair of his chest, her nipples like hard pebbles between them. He wrapped his arms around her back and while he thrust his tongue into her mouth he took over the movement, holding her still while he moved his cock in and out, using the same rhythm she had used. But his tongue pressed into Stephanie's mouth had given her another idea. She broke the kiss and looked around for Gianni. He was sitting on the bed watching their coupling as his hand played with his half-erect cock.

'Come here,' Stephanie ordered. 'I want to suck your cock.'

Gianni knelt on the bed and moved into a position where Stephanie could reach his cock with her mouth. Now it was Devlin's turn to watch as Stephanie's mouth wrapped around Gianni's cock. It was nowhere near hard after his coming. Stephanie could taste her own juices on it, feel the damp pubic hair as she sucked the flaccid organ into her mouth. She knew she could get him hard again. She opened her mouth wider and with the help of her fingers pushed his balls into her mouth too, so she had it all crammed between her lips. The effect was instant. She could feel his flesh swell.

Devlin was moving his cock harder, provoked by what he was seeing. What Stephanie was doing to Gianni in front of his eyes, and what he had already seen was making his control ebb away. With his size he always tried to keep his self-restraint, knowing he could hurt so easily. But now, without realising it, his rhythm was becoming more insistent, his penetration deeper, his ability to be considerate waning away as a red tide of desire began to flow through him.

He saw Gianni's balls pop out of Stephanie's mouth as his cock grew and made it impossible for her to contain them. She lapped hungrily on his cock while her hand reached for his balls. Cupping them in her palm she ground them into the base of his cock in little circular motions. She knew what she wanted. She wanted whatever spunk he had left, wanted it out of his balls and into his cock. She wanted his spunk out of his cock and into her mouth. She wanted spunk in her cunt, in her arse, and in her mouth. The holy trinity. The idea itself brought her off as she thrust her cunt down to meet Devlin's stroke. She thrust her mouth down on Gianni's cock. Another sequence of orgasms was beginning for her just like the last, each one longer, harder, deeper and more intense than the previous one. But this time there were two cocks to provoke them, two cocks wringing the feelings out of her body.

As Devlin's strokes inside her became more insistent, so her mouth sucked more strongly at Gianni. She had no idea if he had any spunk left but if he had she was determined to have it. The three bodies were wrapped in a matrix of feeling with no possible escape. Every movement in one provoked and intensified the movement in the other two. Devlin's cock bucked into Stephanie, Stephanie sucked on Gianni, Gianni felt his spunk rising in his cock, Stephanie felt it swell and pushed down harder on Devlin. Devlin watched Stephanie's mouth and hand working on Gianni, watched her tits hanging down and shaking, the nipples rigid, saw his own penis driving into her ever-open cunt as he looked down between their legs. He reached out and took one of her nipples between thumb and forefinger and pinched it savagely. Gianni did the same. Devlin felt her cunt react, Gianni her mouth; there was a new heat, a new intensity. They pinched again. Had she not been effectively gagged with Gianni's cock Stephanie would have screamed with sheer pleasure.

Gianni was coming. Stephanie could swear, despite his previous orgasm not minutes before, that she could feel his spunk swelling his cock, getting ready to explode. She desperately wanted Devlin's spunk too and wriggled her cunt on him as if to demand action. He replied by thrusting harder and deeper, knowing exactly what she wanted, knowing instinctively she wanted them to spunk together. Gianni knew too and tried to hold back, not understanding how he could be on the verge of orgasm again so soon, but knowing nevertheless that he was, that Stephanie had provoked him to it and that he could not hold back. His cock started to contract as Stephanie's tongue played with the opening in the glans, trying to force its way in there, and the first jet of spunk came right out over her tongue. Devlin saw what was happening and as new gobs of spunk spurted uncontrollably in her mouth Devlin's cock exploded too. He used both his hands on her hips to ram her down on to him, as he arched his back to drive his cock into her. He had no control, there was no holding back, his only concern to get his spunk into that special place he had found deep inside her.

Stephanie's orgasm tore through her body too. Like a musical harmony it seemed perfectly tuned to both men's bodies, each note finding a resonance in the others. Their three bodies came together, their convulsions matching and in tune. But Stephanie had an advantage over the two men. Their orgasm was singular, hers multiple. The shattering climax she had experienced as spunk flooded into her mouth and cunt, as two cocks spasmed inside her, was followed by many aftershocks, not as intense as that the double cocks had produced but orgasms nevertheless. She lay back, her body trembling, spunk in every crevice of her body, feeling higher than she had ever felt in her life. The sudden shock of Devlin's cock finally slipping out of her cunt with an almost audible 'plop' made her come for the last time that night, though she would not have believed herself capable of finding the energy needed once again to moan with pleasure as her body vibrated and shook.

Finally her body was still. The two men lay exhausted, drained, and utterly spent. Wearily, with a great effort, Stephanie got up. She wanted to sleep for what remained of the night in her own room upstairs where there were windows and fresh air. She slipped into a towelling robe (it was Devlin's with the monogrammed pocket) and out of the room. She made her way through the cellars and then up through the deserted castle. Everything was quiet.

In her room she stood on the terrace for a moment letting the cool air wash over her and listening to the stillness and silence of the night. She started to think about what had happened to her, to go over it all and analyse her feelings, but almost immediately a wave of tiredness swept over her. There would be time enough to think about it all in the morning. Now, above all, she needed to sleep.

Walking into the bedroom she took off the robe and slipped between the silk sheets of the bed. She closed her eyes and waited for sleep to arrive, keeping her mind blank, not allowing it to wander off into recollections of any part of her extraordinary day. In seconds she was asleep, a deep, untroubled and, as far as she would remember, dreamless sleep.

Chapter Eleven

Stephanie woke to the sound of church bells. Across the lake on the mainland, in two churches, a bell tolled. Both were tuned to a different pitch. Unlike in England they tolled irregularly, with no particular pattern; sometimes the two sounds coming together, sometimes apart, one a counterpoint for the sound of the other. Stephanie lay and listened, the clear morning air carrying the sound in through the open windows, a slight breeze rustling the material of the curtains.

She got up. Her body felt sore. She was bruised. As she stood under a warm shower she examined the damage. There were bruises on her wrists and ankles where they had been strapped but the straps had been well padded; the bruises were superficial and would soon fade. The weals from the whipping that Gianni had given her had turned from scarlet to deep purple and hurt when she touched them. The one on her inner thigh was the worst, as it was impossible to walk without brushing the other thigh against it. She had good reason to be thankful for Venetia's intervention. Her nipples and clitoris were sore too but that was a different kind of soreness, more a dull ache with not a small measure of pleasure buried in the hurt. They had been pawed and pinched and hammered all day so it was hardly surprising that they felt swollen and sensitive.

Patting herself dry, careful to avoid the whipmarks, Stephanie had only just walked back into the bedroom when there was a knock at her door. Wrapping the bath towel around her body and praying that the visitor was not Gianni or Devlin she opened the door. Her heart lifted when she saw it was Venetia carrying a vast tray of breakfast – coffee, blood-orange juice, croissants and brioches and a plate of sliced melon nestling on a platter of crushed ice.

'I thought you'd like breakfast on your terrace this morning,' Venetia said. She looked fresh but there was a hint of sadness in her eyes.

'You must be psychic. I don't think I'm ready to face Devlin just yet.'

Venetia carried the tray out on to the terrace and laid its contents on to the table, starting with a well-starched white linen tablecloth. She laid two places and poured steaming black coffee for them both. She was wearing a cream silk negligée over a matching nightdress. The nightdress was short, revealing most of her thighs, and a deep inverted V of lace at the front did little to hide her full breasts.

Stephanie, still wrapped in the towel, sat and drank the coffee eagerly, pouring herself a second cup the moment she had finished the first.

'I needed that,' she said. She discovered she was hungry too and applied butter and jam to a croissant.

'We've got a lot to catch up on,' Venetia said. Stephanie looked into Venetia's green eyes. She looked uncertain, as if not sure where last night had left their relationship or indeed what their relationship was. Their experience in London could have been as nothing more than a sexual fling. Stephanie had felt it was more than that but until now there had been no opportunity to discuss it. And what had happened last night had clearly added a new dimension.

'I wanted to . . .'

'Can we . . .'

They both spoke at once, both wanting to clear the air.

'You first,' Stephanie said. Venetia was about to say 'No, you,' but stopped herself.

'I just wanted to say, about last night. I was glad you were there. It helped me,' she said instead.

'Is that true?'

'Yes.'

'I thought I should have tried to stop them.'

'There was nothing you could have done. Nothing.'

'But you tried to help me. If you hadn't . . .'

'That was different. Devlin had no right to do that to you. You were his guest.'

Stephanie wanted to be honest.

'Venetia, I wanted to see what they were going to do to you. I wanted to see it.'

'I know. I saw it in your eyes. It doesn't matter. It was bound to happen sometime. I've been lucky so far. And I've only got myself to blame.'

'You're a . . .' Stephanie could not bring herself to use the word.

'I'm a slave like the rest of them. Did Devlin tell you?'

'Only in general.'

'I worked for his export business. I'm very good with computers. I was in over my head. I'd taken a big mortgage to buy this apartment in Docklands. It had everything. Wooden floors, view over the Thames, jacuzzi in the bathroom, swimming pool and gym in the building, private security, car park. I could manage the mortgage but then I got a bill for the first quarter's service charges. They were ten times what they'd said they would be. I couldn't cope.

So I found a way to divert incoming funds from abroad into my bank account through the computer. It was foolproof. I got away with it for a year.'

The sun had rounded the corner of the castle wall and for the first time that morning Stephanie felt the gentle morning heat on her face.

'And Devlin found out?'

'I got overconfident I suppose. It was too easy. I started taking more than I needed to cover my costs. I bought a new car, new clothes, silk underwear, Gucci handbags. I went completely wild. And someone at work started to take notice. There was this guy who'd always been after me — little weasel with bad breath and crooked teeth. Well, he followed me home one night. Told me if I didn't let him in and sleep with him he was going to tell the managing director where the money came from for all my perks.'

'So what did you do?'

'I threw him out. Next morning I went to see Devlin. I'd never met him. Never even seen him. But I knew he was the overall boss. Chairman of the group that owned our company, all that. So I rang his office and asked if they were expecting him that day. Fortunately they were. I put on my best Valentino dress, best tights, Bally shoes, make-up, the works, and went up to his office. I sat in reception pretending to wait for a friend. I knew they'd never let me in to see him. I had to wait all morning before he finally came out on his way to lunch. I followed him down in the lift and when his chauffeur opened the door of the Rolls I got in ahead of him. Just sat in the back of the car. He was astonished. Then I told him.'

'Told him what?'

'That I'd stolen approximately £750,000 from his company to date.'

'That much?'

'Perhaps a little more. And I told him Bill Giles, the little weasel, wanted to fuck me in return for keeping quiet.' She paused.

'And?'

'He took me to lunch at the Savoy Grill. A very good lunch actually. He asked me how I'd done it. He asked me if I could write a computer programme to prevent it being done again, from any of his companies, since they all used the same mainframe. Then he asked me why I'd come to him direct.'

'And why had you?'

'Because if I was going to be fucked by anyone, especially as I had a preference for women and had never been fucked by a man,' her voice faltered but then she carried on, '. . . it seemed to me it should be him. He thought that was very amusing, I remember. He couldn't stop laughing.'

'So what happened?' Stephanie was intrigued by the story.

'Well, first he fired the little weasel.'

'And then?'

'He told me I wasn't the first. And that he had devised a rather unusual alternative to prosecution and goal.'

'But you didn't go to bed with him?'

Venetia was quiet for a moment remembering things she would rather have forgotten.

'He was involved with a French woman at the time,' she continued. 'She was older, maybe sixty, it was hard to tell. She had one of those tough sun-tanned faces, wore gold jewellery, not an ounce of fat on her body, long painted fingernails, low-heeled shoes, you know the type. Anyway, she had Devlin exactly where she wanted him. He took me to his house . . .' She couldn't help shuddering at the memory.

'She took you to bed?'

'Devlin watched. She was all hard and bony. Not soft like most women. She hurt me. She hurt me more than a man ever could. She wanted to make me pay for what I'd done. And Devlin watched it all. Night after night. It was a long time before she was bored with me.'

'Then you came here?'

'I think Devlin was sorry for me. We came to a sort of agreement. I'd deal with the women and be a sort of roving assistant. That's why I was sent to you.'

Stephanie looked at the beautiful woman who sat in front of her at the table, her long blonde hair flowing over the silk negligée, her breasts half exposed by the lace.

'London was a special experience for me,' Venetia was saying. 'I wouldn't want you to think I did it all the time.'

'I didn't. It was special for me too.' But as she said it Stephanie realised her feelings for Venetia had changed. The events of the last two days had changed them. She still felt affection for her but it was not as complex as it had been when she had ridden down in the lift on Friday expecting Venetia to be outside waiting. Perhaps it was the revelation that Venetia was a slave that was subtly changing the way she felt.

Stephanie sipped more coffee. The early morning sun was surprisingly hot but it was soothing too.

'So why didn't you pick me up on Friday?'

'I wanted to. Something came up.'

'To do with Gianni, no doubt,' Stephanie said allowing a bitter tone into her voice as Gianni's presence seemed to have changed so many plans for his weekend.

'Devlin was in trouble. He overreached himself on a property deal. Borrowed too much to buy it because he thought he had a certain sale worked out. The sale fell through and he was left with all the property and the colossal interest charges. Gianni offered to take the whole thing off his hands. The loans are called in tomorrow. If Devlin can't produce the money . . .'

'And Gianni came through?'
'Apparently.'
'So Devlin's off the hook?'
'And swears he'll never do anything so foolish again.'
'How much did Gianni pay?'
'I don't know exactly.'
'About?' Stephanie persisted.
'A hundred million sterling. Plus all the outstanding charges.'

Stephanie laughed. 'Well if I am going to be treated like a whore, then at least no one can say I was a cheap whore.'

Feeling hot in the sun Stephanie stood up and unwrapped the towel from her body. The weals from the whip were all too visible in the bright sun.

'Do they hurt?'

'This one especially,' Stephanie said parting her legs to show the mark on her inner thigh.

'There's some cream in the bathroom that'll help. I'll get it.' Venetia went inside as Stephanie lay out on the double-width lounger after swinging it out to get the full force of the sun. She touched the two weals on her breasts, so close together they were impossible to distinguish, and felt a sting of pain. The pain was in direct proportion to her anger at Devlin.

Venetia returned carrying a jar of expensive-looking unguent. She stripped off her negligée and knelt on the lounger beside Stephanie.

'This will hurt a little at first,' she said, dipping her fingers into the jar and then spreading the thick white cream as gingerly as she could on to the weals on Stephanie's breasts. Stephanie winced and tears welled up in her eyes but as Venetia's fingertips worked the lotion into her skin the initial stinging effect miraculously gave way to a warm soothing sensation.

'I'm not going to let him get away with it, Venetia,'

Stephanie said as the soothing fingers moved from breast down to thigh. 'I'm going to get my revenge.'

'Your revenge?'

'For drugging me. Using me. Who the hell does he think he is?'

'He had no choice.'

'Don't be ridiculous. I'm his guest. I'm not one of his thieving slaves.' As she blurted the words out she realised at once what she had said. 'I'm sorry. I didn't mean . . .'

'That's all right. It's true, isn't it?'

'Yes. I just . . .'

'I have to live with what I did, Stephanie.'

'I suppose you do. But it doesn't change what he did to me. I can't pretend I didn't enjoy it in the end. Ahh . . .' she winced as Venetia's hand massaged cream into the weal on her inner thigh. 'But I wasn't given any choice. And I told him I was not going to let Gianni near me. Then there's what he did to you. You were only trying to help me. If you hadn't intervened I'd have been covered in these things. No, Venetia, he's going to pay.'

'What can you do?'

'I know exactly what I'm going to do.' Stephanie smiled. Gianni was out of the picture now. It was just her and Devlin. She knew exactly how she was going to make him pay for what he had done to her – payment in kind.

'Open your legs a bit more,' Venetia requested. Stephanie obliged and felt the cream being spread down along her inner thigh. She looked at Venetia's long elegant body, hardly covered by the silk and lace of the short nightdress, her fair hair brushed out and free flowing, shining with health in the sun. She remembered last night and how she had looked in the cellars. She remembered how she had screamed, that thin haunting scream, as she had been penetrated by a man for the first time. Of course, she was right. She had only herself to blame. What had happened last night was her punishment, for interfering with Gianni certainly, but ultimately for what she had done in stealing from Devlin in the first place.

'What happened to Colette?'

'Devlin sent her home. There was a flight this morning first thing.'

'For helping to drug me, I suppose?'

'She didn't have any choice.'

'Oh, I don't blame her. She reminded me of you. I'd like to have spent more time with her.'

'Did you sleep with her?' There was no hint of jealousy in Venetia's voice.

'Briefly. I was trying to use her to get Gianni off my back.'

'He only wanted you.'

'I know. Well, perhaps I'll be able to get my revenge on him too,' Stephanie mused. Devlin was first on her list of priorities, however. Gianni would have to wait.

Venetia took another pat of cream from the jar and directed it to Stephanie's clitoris.

'This is sore too isn't it?'

'Emm . . . That's nice . . .' Venetia's fingers massaged the cream deep into her labia, into her clitoris, right down to the puckered rosebud of her arse. The tender flesh was immediately soothed and relaxed, every hint of soreness smoothed away by Venetia's gentle fingertips and the miracle cream. The warmth of the sun helped too.

'Better?'

'It feels so good.'

'Just enjoy it. Tell me when you've had enough.'

Stephanie reached up to touch Venetia's breast under the cream lace of the nightdress. She could see her nipple through the lace and it was already hard. But Venetia took her hand and put it back by her side, kissing Stephanie lightly on the cheek and whispering:

'This is all for you. Lie back and enjoy it. Don't think about me.'

Stephanie closed her eyes. For a second she had a vision of Colette and wished she had not been sent away. Venetia was applying the cream to each breast in turn, avoiding the weals and massaging the plump flesh and hardening nipple with one hand while the other was circling the knot of Stephanie's clitoris. Stephanie thought of Colette lying on the bed using the dildo on herself, her eyes locked on Stephanie's face. The thick glutinous cream made the contact of flesh on flesh almost frictionless. Venetia's fingers touched her so lightly, so carefully, so tenderly Stephanie almost wanted to cry with delight. This was not the rough wild pleasures of last night, but, by contrast, the pleasure only a woman knows how to give another. Stephanie's mind was full of Colette. She wished she'd taken the dildo, used it on Colette, felt it penetrating her soft wet cunt.

There was no pressure, no need to reach a climax, no need to perform. The continual movement of fingertips on swollen tender parts was end enough in itself. The world seemed to be suspended. Thoughts of Colette faded into the reality of Venetia and the little circles she was making around Stephanie's clitoris. Stephanie thought she was coming but it was so gentle and so quiet, so unlike the orgasms that had torn through her body last night, that it was difficult to be certain. Nor did it matter. What was certain was that the soreness she had woken to this morning had been soothed away.

Stephanie had no need to tell Venetia to stop. She had sensed Stephanie's completion and taken her hands away.

'Feels much better,' Stephanie said, smiling and opening her eyes.

'All part of the service.'

Seeing Venetia kneeling in the short nightdress, her breasts tantalisingly revealed by the lace, her long legs slightly parted, Stephanie felt a rush of desire for this beautiful woman who had made her feel so good. She saw herself leading Venetia into the cool bedroom, lying on the bed with her, kissing her hard on the mouth and pressing her body into Venetia's. But she stopped herself. As always from the moment she had stepped on to the plane, the problem to avoid during the weekend had been overindulgence. There would be time for all that later. Stephanie felt a distance between herself and Venetia now, a distance she welcomed. Not taking her to bed now kept that distance firmly in place.

From below the terrace Stephanie heard the gentle rumble of the motorboat engines. She got up and walked over to the parapet to watch as the boatman skilfully manoeuvred the glimmering metal and polished wood of the boat into position on the jetty. Almost as soon as he'd tied the fore and aft lines, leaving the huge engines idling in the water making a noise like distant thunder, Devlin, Gianni in tow, appeared from under the canopy of leaves and flowers that shrouded the stone steps. Stephanie stepped back slightly into the shade, wanting to see but not be seen. She felt the gentle brush of silk on her naked back as Venetia joined her to peer over her shoulder.

They watched together as Devlin shook hands briskly with Gianni while one of the servants stowed his briefcase aboard the boat. Even from their vantage point on the terrace it was apparent that the relationship between the two men had changed. Devlin was no longer holding himself in a way that suggested, as it had yesterday, his subservience to Gianni. Now his body language was confident and assured. He looked relaxed. Gianni on the other hand exuded an air of tension, shifting his weight from one foot to another, clearly ill at ease and anxious to be off. The boatman helped him into the motorboat and he sat unsmiling on the padded leather seat in the transom. He made no effort to return Devlin's cheery wave as the boatman released the lines and used the boat-hook to ease away from the jetty. As soon as the boat was clear the big engines were gunned into life, a churning white froth appeared as the propellors bit into the water, and the boat surged out over the lake. In seconds Gianni's sullen face merged into the landscape, and in minutes only the huge swathe of wake could be seen.

'Good riddance,' Stephanie commented in relief. The desire she had felt for Gianni last night had in no way affected her overall dislike for the man and she was delighted to see the back of him. But she had every intention of teaching him he couldn't merely snap his fingers and get what he wanted. Gianni's introduction to the cellars and to Stephanie in particular was something that was going to haunt him. He was on the hook now and she had every intention of reeling the line in. But, she told herself, first things first.

'Devlin looks happy,' Venetia said.

'Well, I'll wipe that smile off his face.' Stephanie was smiling to herself at the prospect.

'What are you going to do?'

'I'll explain,' she said, leading Venetia into the bedroom.

Stephanie hadn't bothered with underwear. She wore only her cream silk dress. It buttoned down the front and so was easy to take off again. In fact, she had considered not dressing at all and staying in the robe or a towel, but by the time she had made up carefully, she opted for the dress as it was lighter and cooler. Looking once again at the face that stared back at her from the mirror, she was surprised how little changed it appeared to be. She looked, she had to admit, and despite the vagaries of last night, remarkably fresh and fit. Nothing in her face betrayed what she had experienced or what she had felt. They were to remain her secret.

She had applied her make-up thickly. Once again she knew the impression she wanted to create. She used a dark red lipstick, a thick eyeliner and a lot of mascara on her long eyelashes. Her dark brown eyes stared back at her from the mirror, bright and deep and stern.

If Bruno's face was capable of registering any expression apart from a sort of gloomy disinterest, Stephanie thought, she might have detected a flicker of surprise as he opened the cellar door in response to her impatient knocking. But he had let her in without hesitation and followed her as she had indicated he should.

It felt strange to be back in the punishment room of the cellar suite again, to see the wooden frame where last night she had been strapped and where Venetia had been violated for the first time. But Stephanie was in no mood to dwell on such things. She had come here for a very specific reason. She went to the wardrobes that lined one wall but this time the doors were locked.

'Open them all, Bruno,' she ordered and Bruno obeyed immediately, selecting one key from the many on the ring he always carried at his waist and opening each wardrobe in turn.

As Bruno swung the doors back Stephanie could see the racks of clothing neatly arranged in racks of rubber, leather and oversized women's clothing (clearly intended for the use of men) as well as the drawers of underwear. There were two drawers of bras, two of knickers, two of stockings, and so on. One drawer contained the usual female sizes and one the over-sized versions of the same thing.

Venetia arrived as Stephanie began rifling the wardrobes for the outfit she had in mind. She had changed into a duck-blue tracksuit.

'How about this?' Stephanie asked, unhooking a red leather basque from the rail.

'Black's better on you,' Venetia said. She rummaged around until she found the identical item in black. Then she helped Stephanie off with her dress.

'Let's see.' Stephanie held the cold leather against her naked body and looked into one of the mirrors that lined the wardrobe doors. She noticed Bruno still standing by the door, his arms once again folded over his chest, his eyes firmly fixed on her body. She wondered, momentarily, if whatever accident he had suffered had after all left him completely disinterested, as Devlin had seemed to believe.

'I'll do it up.' Venetia came round and started hooking up the long row of fastenings at the back. 'Breathe in,' she said as she got to the tight sculptured waist.

The basque fitted perfectly. The soft leather moulded itself to Stephanie's body, the half-cup bra giving a tantalising glimpse of her firm breasts and more than a hint of nipple, the pinched waist emphasising the flare and curve of her rounded hips and buttocks. Stephanie found a pair of knickers, no more than a G-string, made from the same soft leather. She stepped into them, then sat on the wooden frame and rolled a pair of sheer black stockings over her legs, smoothing them out before clipping them into the suspenders of the basque.

'Find me a pair of boots with high heels,' she said as the first stocking was clipped into place. She watched Bruno's eyes following her hands as they unrolled the sheer nylon over her creamy flesh.

'How about these?' Venetia asked, holding a pair of black boots.

'Not high enough.'

'These, then,' Venetia said. They were perfect, the heels adding four inches to Stephanie's height. She would tower over Devlin now.

'What shall I wear, then?' Venetia pulled off her tracksuit.

'The red basque. It's better with your hair.'

Venetia pulled the red leather around her body while Stephanie hooked her into it. It was a little small for Venetia, the half-bra especially struggling to contain Venetia's voluptuous breasts. Her outfit was completed by red stockings, a pair of silk knickers and red high-heeled shoes rather than boots. Stephanie made Venetia change the first pair of shoes she tried, as they made her taller than Stephanie and she didn't want that. Not today. Not for what she had in mind.

It took Stephanie a few minutes to choose a whip from the display on the wall. She noticed that the one Gianni had used on her the night before had been replaced in its mounting. Trying several for weight and balance she swished them through the air inches from where Bruno was standing impassively. He did not flinch. Finally she chose a heavy riding crop with a plaited leather handle tipped with a broad loop of black leather.

'Shall I try it out on you?' she said to Venetia, unable to keep a slight tone of menace out of her voice. She realised she would actually have liked to use it on Venetia, to see the other woman bend down, her arse unprotected by the thin string of the knickers, and watch as the crop whacked against her soft plump flesh. After all, she could do precisely what she wanted to do with Venetia. She was a slave too. Perhaps her eyes betrayed what she was thinking. Venetia was suddenly cold and frightened.

'You can if you want to,' she said reluctantly.

'I know,' Stephanie said frostily. For a moment they were not two equals, but mistress and slave.

The moment passed. Stephanie decided she must not be distracted. As ever that was the problem with the castle, too many possibilities, too many indulgences. This morning

Stephanie could so easily have taken Venetia to bed. The idea of feeling that long body pressed into hers was so tempting. And now, seeing Venetia dressed so provocatively, she could easily have had Bruno tie her down to one of the punishment frames. She could have used her and abused her and enjoyed every minute of it. But it was a question of priorities and the number one item on the agenda today was Devlin. Stephanie had no intention of forgetting that. No one, however rich and powerful, was going to treat her like an object, a piece of property to be used at whim, whatever the financial stakes. That was the lesson she was going to teach Devlin and one he would never be allowed to forget. Everything else could wait.

Chapter Twelve

The clatter of high heels on the marble floor of the long hall at the top of the cellar steps echoed through the castle. A white-coated servant appeared to see if he might be of service, only to scurry away at the sight of the two formidably dressed women striding purposefully into the main reception room. Apart from him, however, the castle appeared to be quiet and seemingly deserted. There was no sign of Devlin in any of the reception rooms.

'He's probably in the office,' Venetia volunteered, leading the way back into the hall and down a long passage Stephanie had not noticed before, behind the main staircase. Once again the clatter of heels on the polished marble, like the staccato sound of machine-gun fire, sounded out through the building.

At the end of the corridor Venetia stopped in front of a small wooden door delicately carved with ornate gothic panels.

'In here,' she said.

'OK. You go and arrange things downstairs,' Stephanie instructed, adjusting the whip in her hand. 'You know what to do.'

'I'll be ready.'

She was about to turn and go when Stephanie's voice stopped her.

'Venetia . . .' She let the name hang in the air between them.

'Yes?'

'I want to spend some time alone with you later. Just the two of us.'

'I'd like that very much.'

Stephanie leant forward and kissed Venetia fleetingly on the cheek before her attitude of authority returned.

'Off you go then.'

As Venetia returned to the cellars Stephanie turned the handle of the office door as quietly as she could and tiptoed into the room beyond. She found herself in a large office lined with white filing cabinets and shelves of computer tapes. There were three secretaries' desks, each with computer terminals, telephones and VDUs, but none was occupied. In one corner of the room Stephanie could see a glass door and beyond another office which clearly belonged to Devlin.

Threading her way silently past the fax machine, paper shredder and desks she walked towards the glass door. Through it she saw that the second office was very differently arranged. There were no filing cabinets, no computers, no files, just a massive desk carved from a single piece of walnut, a long low leather sofa of an ultra-modern design, and two other chairs, one in front of the desk and one behind. On the desk there was a single telephone and very little else. A small cabinet underneath it probably held other office items neatly stored away. Devlin was obviously a very tidy man.

A long picture window had been cut in the solid stone and Stephanie could see the view of the castle's walled gardens and orchards on the other side of the island where she had been yesterday. The sun was still at the front of the castle so most of the walled garden was in shade.

At first this office too appeared to be deserted. Stephanie was right in front of the glass door now and suddenly heard Devlin's voice. It took her a moment to realise that he must be sitting in the desk chair swivelled around to face the window, its leather back completely obscuring him from view.

Stephanie took a deep breath and strode into the office.

'Everything's organised,' Devlin was saying into the phone. 'It's all taken care of. You can stop worrying. No problems, Bob. Check with the bank as soon as they open. The money'll be there.'

'Put the phone down,' Stephanie barked, surprised at how hard her voice sounded.

Devlin swung the chair round. He put his hand over the mouthpiece while his eyes surveyed her body with obvious delight.

'Just a minute . . .'

'Now!' Stephanie commanded. In a fluid movement she brought the riding crop down to slap across the desk. It missed Devlin's fingers by a quarter of an inch. He put the phone down without a word.

'That's better.'

'My darling, you look magnificent. As always you surprise me. You are a most remarkable woman.'

'I am not your darling. Not after last night.'

'I know, I know. I was just coming to talk to you about it. It was unforgivable, unconscionable. I invited you here as my guest. I hoped we'd have a wonderful weekend. But this thing with Gianni . . . I was in terrible trouble, my dear.'

'I don't want your excuses.'

'It's all over now. I will make it up to you.'

'Shut up.'

'Anything, Stephanie. My God, you look so wonderful . . .'

'Shut up, I said!' The second blow of the crop hit Devlin squarely on the hand. He yelped like a little dog. 'Come over here,' she said, indicating a space in front of the desk.

Devlin got up slowly; he seemed to realise that this was not some new game – there was genuine anger in Stephanie's eyes. He rounded the desk and stood in front of her. In the heels she was a foot taller than him.

'Turn round,' she ordered. He obeyed.

She'd kept her left hand behind her back since she'd entered Devlin's office. She hadn't wanted him to see the handcuffs she'd brought up from the cellars.

'Put your hands behind your back.'

Again he obeyed. She quickly snapped the cold steel around his wrists, not caring that he winced as she clamped them too tightly in place.

'That's better.' Stephanie walked around the desk and slid into the high-backed leather chair, putting her boots up on the desk and rocking back in the chair.

'Very comfortable. This is where you wheel and deal, is it? This is where you get yourself into trouble. Venetia tells me Gianni paid quite a high price for the privilege of using me. Is that right?'

'It wasn't really like . . .'

'Is that right?' Stephanie slapped the crop down on the desk again, making Devlin flinch.

'Yes.'

'Good, because I'm going to make you pay a high price too.'

The heels of her boots were pointed straight at Devlin. Stephanie could see his eyes furtively darting over her body, her long legs, the taut suspenders, her half-exposed nipples and the diminutive crotch of the G-string knickers which, she knew, did little to conceal the thick pubic hair at the slit of her sex. She wanted him to see it.

'You are very beautiful,' he said tentatively.

'I don't want to hear what you think. Keep your mouth shut.' Her voice was angry; she felt cold and calculating. She was in control. She was going to use her anger. If what had happened to her last night had not, overall, been such a sensual experience, she would have felt very differently. Her anger would have been hot and uncontrollable. As it was, she could allow herself to feel just sufficient outrage to make her anger at Devlin real and nasty, while at the same time knowing what he had done to her was no more than an extension of what she had allowed to happen, with her full consent, on Friday night. She was certainly not going to tell Devlin that, not now and maybe not ever. Now she was going thoroughly to enjoy the moral high ground. With his hands cuffed behind his back and her high heels giving her new authority she could enjoy the physical high ground too.

'We're going down to the cellars,' she announced, swinging her legs off the desk and getting up. She walked around the room poking at the various *objets d'art*, picking up the little pieces of sculpture that served as Devlin's executive toys. 'You're going to make sure Bruno doesn't interfere and then, Devlin, I'm going to make you pay the price for treating me as if I was one of your thieving little slaves. Because you don't seem to think there's any difference, do you?'

Devlin did not reply. Stephanie, who was a few feet behind him now, lashed out with the crop. It caught him a stinging blow across the top of his thighs and he cried out in pain.

'Do you?'

'No.'

'And there is one other thing, Devlin. You are to take

no action against Venetia. She tried to help me last night and you punished her for it. Well, I think she's entitled to a little revenge too, don't you?'

'I tried to explain she's just a ...'

'Don't you?' Stephanie lashed the crop across his upper arm.

'Yes.'

'And then it will be forgotten, won't it? Completely forgotten.' Devlin nodded. 'Say it!'

'It will be forgotten.'

'That's better.' She paused and walked over to the picture window, standing with her back to Devlin, her legs apart. She knew he would be staring at her arse, perfectly framed at the top by the black leather of the basque, at the sides by the suspenders and at the bottom by the thick black welts of the stocking tops. It would look firm and tight, a ripe peach split in two by the leather thong of the G-string.

'Well, I think it's time to take a little walk now, Devlin.'

Stephanie grabbed Devlin's tie, a very expensive Sulka silk tie which he would never be able to wear again, and pulled Devlin forward like a dog on a lead. He had to stoop forward as he walked, his head pulled down by the tie. She led him out of the office, through the long corridor and down into the cellars. As he walked she could not help noticing the huge bulge in front of his dark blue cotton trousers. She had certainly improved Devlin's ability to achieve spontaneous erections since her arrival at the castle. She made sure Devlin did not see her smile.

In the cellars Venetia had been busy. Though most of the slave cells were small, the two at the far end of the brick-vaulted corridor, the end that contained the cellar suite, were slightly bigger – big enough, at least, for Stephanie's plan. Using the authority Devlin had given her over the years and which Bruno had never failed to recognise without question Venetia had ordered Bruno to assemble all the slaves in one of the larger cells. There were nine now that Colette had gone, not including the masked man. He was left in his cell. Stephanie and Venetia had very special plans for him.

Bruno opened each cell in turn, unlocked the ankle chain from the ring in the floor of the cell and led the slave to the larger chamber. Instead of having all the chains locked to the ring in the floor of that cell, Bruno merely locked the chain of one slave to the ankle-cuff of another so that only the original inhabitant of the larger cell was secured to the floor ring. All the others were secured to him in line. During their time at the castle none of the slaves had experienced any manoeuvres of this sort, but knowing Bruno's attitude to unsolicited conversation and seeing his whip hanging as ever at his side, none of them broke the silence.

It had taken some time to accomplish the rearrangement. Bruno was still attaching the last chain when Stephanie knocked at the outer door and Venetia let her in.

'Everything ready?' Stephanie asked, pulling Devlin forward by the tie.

'Bruno's just doing the last one.'

'Well Devlin has been very understanding. You're free to help me. Then it'll be forgotten. Right, Devlin?'

'Yes. Absolutely.'

'This way.' Stephanie pulled on the tie again and Devlin followed her down to the end of the corridor. Bruno had finished his labours and was tucking the keyring back into his belt. He looked puzzled when he saw Devlin's position, hands cuffed behind his back, pulled along by his tie.

'Say it,' Stephanie prompted.

'You can go, Bruno,' Devlin muttered. 'Take some time off.'

'Out of the cellars,' she prompted again.

'Out of the cellars,' Devlin repeated.

Bruno looked uncertain. Stephanie picked the bunch of keys from his belt. Instantly his hand flew out and caught her by the wrist in a vicelike grip.

'Devlin . . .' she said, unable to break the grip by herself.

'Give her the keys, Bruno,' he said. 'Then go. It's all right. Just go.'

Stephanie could see Bruno trying to work out what he should do. Suddenly he released her wrist, emitted an audible grunt of displeasure, the first noise Stephanie had heard him make, and, with obvious reluctance, sloped off down the corridor. When he reached the main door he looked back as if expecting Devlin to change his mind. As Devlin remained silent he swung the heavy door open and made his exit slamming the door shut after him. The noise echoed through the cellars. Venetia quickly bolted the door from the inside.

'Now it's just us, Devlin. No one to help you.'

Pulling on his tie again Stephanie led Devlin into the far cell. The assembled slaves did not react to the sight of their master being led in like a dog. Most of them had been at the castle long enough to know that anything could happen. To them it was just another game, probably devised by the master himself, in which no doubt their collective role would be, as it always was ultimately in the cellars, a form of punishment.

When Devlin reached the centre of the room Stephanie dropped the tie.

'Take your clothes off,' she ordered.

'I can't,' Devlin said.

'Why not?' Stephanie demanded. She reached forward, flicked open the top button of his trousers and pulled the zip of his flies, with some difficulty, over the bulge of his erection which had been maintained all the way down from the offices. The trousers fell to his ankles. His white boxer shorts were not able to contain the length of his cock and it poked out from the vent in the front. 'Why not?' Stephanie repeated, sending a swingeing cut from the whip to land on the side of Devlin's bare thigh.

With difficulty he managed to hook his fingers into the elastic at the waist of the boxer shorts at the back and pull them down to his knees. Then he shook his legs until they fell around his ankles, on top of his trousers. His shirt-tails hid his buttocks but at the front his erection jutted up unencumbered.

'Come on,' Stephanie goaded him, tapping him with the crop on the back of his knee. The slaves watched impassively as Devlin tried to get his feet extracted from his trousers and shorts without the help of his hands and while still wearing shoes. It was not a dignified exercise but after much effort he managed it. He stood in shirt, shoes and socks.

Stephanie looked at the slaves for their reaction but if she was expecting them to be showing their amusement she was disappointed. None of them wanted to give Devlin reason for punishments later. Among the faces she recognised Norman, the Rubenesque woman whom she and Devlin had used the first morning, and the stocky man she had used in turn. The two men from her first night at the castle were there too, the only other men among the slaves. The rest were women. As was the practice in the cells the women were all naked, the men naked but for the hard leather pouches locked around their genitals.

Venetia had found a large pair of scissors and was cheerfully cutting off Devlin's expensive hand-made shirt. She cut all the way up the back and through the collar until the shirt fell away in two pieces. She slit the sleeves, each in turn, until the pieces fell away from his arms. Then she knelt by his feet and, as he stood precariously on one foot, unable to use his arms for balance, she slipped off his shoes and socks. Devlin was naked, his massive erection quivering in front of him.

'On your knees, then,' Stephanie commanded, bringing the crop down hard on his left buttock, making him yelp. He got to his knees again, finding this difficult without the use of his arms. 'Now this is your first lesson. I want you to tell them how sorry you are for the way you treated me. You are sorry, aren't you?'

'Yes.'

'Say it, then.'

'I'm very sorry for the way I treated you.'

'You don't *sound* very sorry,' Stephanie said.

'I am very sorry,' he repeated trying to sound more penitent.

'How did you treat me, Devlin?'

'I don't understand.' He looked puzzled.

'You treated me appallingly, didn't you?' She lashed out with the whip, hitting him squarely on his naked buttocks.

'Oh yes, yes. Appallingly,' he said quickly.

'Now everyone in this room is going to use the crop on you.' As Stephanie said it she heard a murmur from the slaves. 'They are going to remember how they have been abused by you and they are, for once, going to be allowed to get their own back. And you will take no action against them later. Is that understood?'

'Yes,' he mumbled.

'They didn't hear you, Devlin.'

'Yes.'

'Yes, what?' she insisted.

'I won't take any action against them later.'

Stephanie had not taken her eyes off Devlin during this exchange. A tear of fluid had formed on his cock, an obvious indication of his excitement. She doubted anyone had given him this treatment before, or that he had ever imagined it was something that would turn him on. But clearly it did. His erection, always huge, now seemed massive. His gnarled and rutted cock, each blood vessel and vein swollen and prominent seemed to be alive, twitching and throbbing, eager, no doubt, to be touched and held.

Stephanie handed the whip to one of the male slaves first.

'Touch your forehead to the floor, Devlin. And keep it there.'

He obeyed instantly, even, Stephanie thought, willingly, thrusting his arse into the air. Stephanie nodded for the slave to begin and he lashed the crop across Devlin's prone arse. Devlin moaned but the stroke was not hard.

'You'd better do it again or I'll use the whip on you,' Stephanie told him.

The slave stood back, raised his arm in the air and this time lashed the crop on to Devlin's body missing the middle of his arse but hitting the upper region where it joined his back. Devlin screamed. A thin red weal appeared immediately on his white skin.

'That's much better.'

Stephanie handed the whip on. Two more slaves laid blows on their master but with no particular enthusiasm. It was when she handed the whip to Norman, the slave who had oiled her on the terrace, that she saw a sign of real pleasure. He obviously remembered a humiliation at Devlin's hands that he was only too happy to redress. He raised the whip high and measured his stroke first, like a golfer practising his drive, before he let the whip fly, whistling through the air to land high on Devlin's rump. The pain made Devlin scream and for a second, though only a second, he rocked back on his haunches, head up, as though not prepared to take any more.

'Get your head down. I think such enterprise deserves a reward. You get a second go, Norman.'

Devlin hesitated before resting his head back on the cold stone floor. He touched his forehead to the stone again. If anything, Norman's second attempt was harder, the crop searing into Devlin's flesh, creating a straight line of pain. But it was a pain that Stephanie knew was feeding Devlin's pleasure.

Each slave stepped forward in turn, their ankle chains clanging against the floor. The Rubenesque woman hit him hard too, putting her weight behind the stroke, her body trembling with the effort. Another of the women slaves delivered a massive blow, perhaps the hardest of them all, and Stephanie had thought she heard the woman murmur 'You bastard', as the crop came down. But though Devlin screamed he did not raise his head again. Ten strokes in all, not counting the first slave's weak attempt. Ten red-hot weals crisscrossed over Devlin's once white arse. Stephanie thought she could feel the heat it was producing. What Devlin would have given to be able to soothe it with his, or somebody else's, cool hands.

'What do you say, Devlin?' Stephanie prodded him with her foot.

'What do you want me to say?' he replied, puzzled. She swung the crop, which she had taken from the last slave, and hit his arm held behind his back by the cuffs.

'Don't be insolent. You say thank you.'

'Thank you,' he said quickly to avoid another blow.

'Now you are going to crawl over and lick my boots, Devlin. Lick every inch of my boots for what you did to me.'

Stephanie handed the crop to Venetia. The bed in the cell was by the door. Stephanie sat on it and crossed her legs.

'Come on then.'

Devlin inched his way forward on his knees. It was difficult shuffling along without the use of his hands and the stone scratched his knees which were bearing all his weight. As Stephanie watched him she was suddenly aware of the level of her own excitement. Her nipples, barely contained in the half-cup bra of the basque, were rigid and tight. Her cunt was so wet that her juices would be only too obvious behind the thin strap of the G-string.

'Faster, Devlin.' She nodded to Venetia who let the crop fall on Devlin's already tortured buttocks. Devlin wriggled forward trying to obey, his cock constantly banging against his navel.

It was not only the sight of his massive cock that was exciting Stephanie. It was not only the knowledge that she could have him fuck her, suck her, wank her or do anything else she desired that was sending her pulse racing. That was part of it, of course. Here in this room there was every imaginable sexual opportunity. She could have herself serviced in ways she had not imagined – and she had a very fertile imagination. She was in control, she was calling the shots, she was in charge. She could make Devlin do whatever *she* wanted him to do. The power made every part of her body hum like an electric dynamo.

Devlin reached the bed. He moved to lick the left boot as it dangled in the air but as his tongue projected from his mouth Stephanie recrossed her legs. He moved to the side to reach the right foot scraping his knees again. Again Stephanie recrossed her legs putting the left foot back in its original position, danging in midair. Devlin moved back and this time Stephanie allowed his tongue to make contact with the leather.

'No, Devlin. Lick the soles.' She made no effort to present the soles to his mouth. Venetia used the crop to reinforce the message. He twisted round to get his mouth turned upward on to the sole of Stephanie's boot.

He licked the dry leather sole over and over again. Though Stephanie could feel no physical contact through the leather, the pace of her arousal had quickened appreciably as she watched Devlin strain to keep his mouth in position. She had never seen his erection so hard.

Stephanie recrossed her legs and presented her right boot for treatment. Devlin resumed his work immediately, Venetia standing over him, waiting to punish any slackening with the whip. The whole of his buttocks were red now, the whip marks beginning to turn scarlet. He was moving his arse from side to side, perhaps trying to get some comfort from the cooling effect of the air. It clearly wasn't helping much.

The slaves were all watching intently, knowing now that this was not a game and especially not a game of Devlin's devising. One of the women slaves had her hand between her legs and was stroking herself, unconscious, probably, of what she was doing. None of the male slaves with their tight leather pouches had any such relief available to them.

Devlin continued to lick. When Stephanie ordered him to lick the little steel heel of the boot he did so. When she ordered him to take the whole heel into his mouth and suck it he did so. When she relented slightly and allowed him to lick the softer leather of the upper boot he did so again, now able to see the length and curves of Stephanie's crossed legs. He would be able to see her crotch clearly, bisected by the strap of the G-string, the pubic hair matted and wet.

Stephanie moved her boot from Devlin's mouth on to his shoulder and pushed. He went sprawling on to the floor.

'That's enough.'

She lay back on the bed and pulled the G-string down her legs and off. She unzipped the boots and threw them on the floor.

'You are not allowed to come, Devlin. Is that understood?'

'Yes,' he said uncertainly.

'Good. Now lick my cunt.'

As he scrambled to his feet his erection jutted from his body.

She opened her legs and imagined she felt a rush of juices escaping from her open labia, where before they had been pressed together. As Devlin struggled to position himself between her legs Stephanie dipped a finger into her cunt. It was soaking wet. She used the same hand to pull Devlin's head down on to her cunt and hold it there. Kneeling as he was, his hands cuffed in the small of his back, it was difficult for him to get his mouth into the right position but with a few adjustments he managed it. His tongue felt good, thick and rough against her clitoris. The first contact was enough, in her state of arousal, to make her gasp with pleasure. But that was only the beginning. As she thrust her hips up off the bed to give Devlin better access to her sex she nodded at Venetia who immediately brought the crop down on Devlin's exposed rump. His scream was gagged by Stephanie's cunt but she felt it, felt the hot air explode from his mouth. Venetia hit again, and again the scream was felt but not heard. None of Venetia's strokes were faint: this was her revenge and Stephanie could see in her eyes she was going to enjoy every minute of it.

Stephanie had never felt a hotter mouth and tongue on her cunt. It was as though he was breathing fire. His saliva mixed with her copious juices. The third lash made her come as another scream was muffled by her cunt. She came over his face, feeling as if she was spraying his face with her juices. Devlin could hear Venetia preparing for a fourth blow.

'Please, no more. I can't take it,' he begged, pulling his mouth away from Stephanie's cunt far enough to get the words out.

'I like to hear you beg,' Stephanie said, the aftermath of her orgasm still rolling through her body. 'Let them all hear.'

'Please, no more. Please!' Devlin cried.

'Again.'

'Please, please, please,' he begged.

She pushed his mouth back down on to her cunt. She could feel herself coming again. Hearing him beg was making her come. She wanted that hot rough tongue on her clitoris. But she wanted those huge fingers inside her too and that massive cock. She wanted to feel everything now, to see and feel everything, to take herself, even by the standards of this weekend, to heights she had never been to before. Her second orgasm was sharp, almost painful, as these thoughts and Devlin's tongue brought her off.

'Uncuff him,' she ordered. Venetia found the key and quickly released his hands. 'Now wank me Devlin.'

There was no time to massage his sore wrists. He rolled on to his side, avoiding any pressure on his whipped and smarting arse, and pushed his finger deep into Stephanie's wet cunt, grateful at least that his shoulders were no longer restrained by the cuffs. He could see Venetia pulling her tiny red knickers down her long stockinged legs and stepping out of them. She too was already wet, her sparse pubic hair revealing glistening labia.

Stephanie was moaning as he used his finger as a penis, driving it in and out of her. Venetia positioned herself over Stephanie's mouth, slowly lowering her cunt on to it. Devlin increased the speed of his penetrations. He could see Stephanie's tongue darting between Venetia's labia, thrusting on to her clitoris. Out of the corner of his eye he caught another movement as the male slaves edged forward. At first he thought it was to get a better view but then he realised Bruno's keys lay on the floor by the bed. The keys to all the leather pouches were in that bunch.

Venetia came quickly, glad, after last night, to feel a woman again, especially this woman. Stephanie probed Venetia's cunt using her tongue to wank her clitoris from side to side, then pushing it deep between her labia, to literally lap up the juices that were running down into her mouth.

Stephanie wanted only one thing. She wanted Devlin's cock. She pulled herself out from between Venetia's legs. As she came up for air she saw Norman had Bruno's keyring in his hand and was unlocking one of the slaves' genital pouches. For half a second she thought of ordering them to stop but she was too concerned with her own pleasure to be bothered. She hadn't time for anything else.

She turned on her stomach and raised herself on her knees, thrusting her bum into the air.

'Fuck me Devlin.'

He fell on her like a lion. The huge cock sunk deep into her wet cunt, deeper than it had ever been before, because Stephanie had never been so open, so voracious. However often she experienced the first thrust of his cock she knew she would never get used to it. It filled her body and filled her mind. It dominated her. It took her over. She had to struggle with herself to get back into control. As always the first thrust brought her to orgasm. As the orgasm receded she fought with herself to regain her dominance.

On his fourth stroke into her she came again, but this time she was in control. She allowed herself to come. She allowed herself to start the process of continual orgasm that she had experienced before with Devlin. Wriggling herself back on his cock she felt every inch of it and tried to get it deeper into her. But it was impossible. She contracted her cunt on his cock, squeezing it as hard as she could; then she relaxed opening herself again like a flower blossoming in time-lapse photography.

Venetia lay on the bed next to her. Stephanie turned

her head to kiss her. Stephanie's mouth tasted of Venetia's juices. Their tongues circled each other, Venetia licking up her own taste from Stephanie's mouth. Venetia found one of Stephanie's nipples and pinched it hard between thumb and forefinger, letting the nail of her thumb bite into the soft corrugated flesh, and producing a moan from Stephanie. But it was enough to send another shuddering climax through Stephanie's body. Venetia could feel it on her tongue, Devlin on his cock, the reverbations like an echo in a mountain pass.

Breaking the kiss Venetia continued to work on Stephanie's nipple, pulling the bra of the basque completely clear of both her breasts. She sent her other hand down between her own legs. Her clitoris was swollen and hot, wanting attention, feeling neglected. She wanked it aggressively, hard and fast as if she were strumming a guitar, and brought herself off immediately as she watched Devlin's cock plunging into Stephanie's cunt.

Stephanie watched Venetia too. The sight of this beautiful woman masturbating so blatantly was yet another sexual spur. She turned her head in the other direction to look at the slaves. For a moment she could not understand what she was seeing. Instead of standing obediently in a neat line by the wall of the cell, the slaves were now a mass of bodies, coupled, interlinked intertwined, their ankle chains little impediment to their actions. It was impossible to tell who was doing what to whom. The genital pouches lay discarded on the floor. She turned away.

'You're not to come, Devlin,' she barked, amazed at her own control. She wanted to feel Devlin's spunk more than anything she could imagine. He was hammering into her harder now, his penis swollen and wanting its fulfilment.

'Please.'

'No,' she said wriggling back on his cock, her words contradicting her actions. He pumped harder.

'Please.'

'Beg me, Devlin. I want to hear you beg me.' The words made her come. The idea made her come. She wanted to hear him beg, beg to be allowed to spunk, beg to be allowed to use her cunt.

'I beg you.'

She was still coming as the head of his cock crashed deep into her womb, her body out of control but her mind still able to function.

'Again.'

'I beg you, I beg you.' He sounded like a little boy about to burst into tears. 'I beg you . . .'

Stephanie came again and again. It was impossible to tell where one orgasm began and the last one ended. She was shaking all over. Her eyes rolled back in her head; she was unable to do anything now but experience her orgasms. Devlin, with all his power and wealth, was begging her like a little boy to be allowed to come. She knew that when she ordered him to come his spunk would jet into her, flood her, fill her, his cock swelling as he came.

'Shall I take my cunt away?' she taunted, wanting to hear him once more. She was just able to stop her body moving with his but knew she would not be able to hold still for long.

'No, no, please.' There was real alarm in his voice that she might actually carry out the threat, take away from him the thing he most desired, deny him what every nerve in his body ached and craved for. He was so close to his climax now he would spend in midair if she pulled away.

Stephanie's body suddenly released a flood of juices. It cascaded over his prick. She could feel it literally running out of her cunt as though she had spunked. She opened her eyes and looked at Venetia, who was coming on her own hand again as she watched Devlin's cock held firm by Stephanie's cunt.

'What do you want?' Her body would not allow her to remain still any longer. It bucked down on his cock, increasing the rhythm again. 'Say it.'

'I want to spunk.' She could hear the desperation in his voice.

'Come then. Give it to me, you bastard!' The words launched her into another climax but she knew it would not be the last. She could feel Devlin's cock moving differently now, freed at last from the need to hold back. She moaned as she felt it swell, as it filled every inch of her soaking wet cunt, as it made its final penetration searching for the place to spunk. She felt it ease back slightly to give itself room to jet the spunk into her, spunk that nothing could hold back now. If she threw herself forward at this moment, pulled his cock out of her body he would not be able to stop himself coming. That would be his final punishment. But she was trapped. She could not do it. She had to have his spunk inside her; she had to.

His cock bucked and he came. His cock pulsed as each separate gob of spunk jetted out from its tip. In her mind's eye Stephanie could see it, white-hot spunk pumping out of him. She heard herself scream as her body took control now and carried her to a last shattering orgasm. Everything that had preceded it made this one higher, deeper and more intense. It was as if all the other orgasms she had had were still in her, and now came back to combine in a sexual climax that wracked through the furthest recesses of her body, leaving no nerve, no feeling, no sense untouched. She was moaning, screaming, babbling, her whole body throbbing with sexual energy, as it twisted and shook to wring every last drop of feeling from her climax.

She collapsed down from her knees with Devlin on top of her. It was a long time before the involuntary movements of her body, each one like an orgasm in miniature, subsided, and even longer before they stopped altogether.

Devlin rolled off her and Venetia leant over to kiss her softly on the lips. It was such a tender kiss it almost made Stephanie want to come again. But only almost.

Chapter Thirteen

Stephanie luxuriated in the warm water of the bath. She had laced it with expensive bath oil and the water felt silky and soothing as it lapped around her body. On the thick marble ledge that enclosed the bathtub she had had one of the servants place a silver wine-cooler containing a well-chilled bottle of Krug, her favourite champagne. She had ordered caviar too, a delicacy she adored but could seldom afford. This now sat next to the champagne, a whole tin of the best Beluga slotted into a specially made crystal glass and silver server surrounded with all the usual trimmings – chopped egg, onion, capers – and wafers of fresh Melba toast. In fact, she ate the caviar unadorned, scraping teaspoons of the stuff on to the toast, enjoying the extravagance and conscious that she was suddenly very hungry.

Totally relaxed, she filled the champagne flute again and sipped at the chilled wine. True, her body was sore in places, but that was not surprising considering what she had put it through over the last three days. But it was not an unpleasant soreness, rather a dull ache. For once her nipples were flaccid, their flesh retracted into the gentle curve of her firm breasts. She looked down at them, the water just covering their lower half, its edge lapping at the higher slopes like the shore of a lake by a hillside.

Looking at herself in the mirror she saw that she was smiling. As she watched the smile broke into a wide and foolish grin. She made a face at herself in the mirror, wrinkling her face up and sticking out her tongue. Why shouldn't she be happy? Here she was in an exotic castle, surrounded by every conceivable luxury – its future secured due in no small measure to herself – and able to call for anything her heart desired merely by picking up the telephone. Limousines, private airplanes, motorboats, clothes, silk and lace underwear, all at her disposal. White-coated servants to fulfil her slightest caprice.

Back in London, when she and Devlin had first met, he had needed very special stimuli before he was able to fuck her properly. Here in the castle he had admittedly taken the lead but somewhere she had picked out the thread of his sexuality and woven it into her own. On Friday it had been his scenario they enacted, and he had been slow to get an erection. By Saturday she had started to understand what he wanted – though by no means consciously – and she had given him an erection in the bathroom as well as among the elaborate paraphernalia of the punishment room. It was not vanity on her part; she knew no other woman had ever done this for Devlin. She could see it in his eyes. As they had cleared the slaves out of the cell with Bruno's help she had seen Devlin was completely dazed. Though it was intended as punishment she had always known, instinctively, that for Devlin the punishment would not be unwelcome. What she had not realised was quite to what extent she had tapped a nerve in Devlin's complex sexual psyche. But that was undoubtedly precisely what she had done. And he knew it.

She had come to realise how closely pain and pleasure were related. She only had to look down at the red weal across her breasts, fading now but still visible, to understand that. Of course, it was a special kind of pain. It was pain by consent, almost pain by invitation. No one would be turned on by real pain. But pain by consent was an entirely different matter. She had no doubt it was an implicit part of her own sexuality and undoubtedly of Devlin's. Masochism and sadism were two sides of the same coin. But it was the same coin. To give and to receive. She'd wanted to give and he'd wanted to receive. And vice versa. Perhaps not exactly vice versa, but close enough. She could not pretend she had not enjoyed the intervals of submission.

She put the champagne flute down and sank back into the water. The bathtub was so big that she could submerge herself totally in the water, enjoying the feeling of it washing over her face and hair as she held her breath. In her tub at home she could barely straighten her legs in a sitting position. She surfaced breathing out as the water streamed out of her hair and down over her body. In the mirror she saw her black hair, plastered down over her head by the water making her appear rather masculine, emphasising the strong bone structure of her face.

She heard a tentative knock at the bedroom door.

'Who is it?' she shouted.

'Devlin.'

'Come in.'

She heard the bedroom door open and Devlin enter.

'I'm in the bath,' she said.

'Is it all right if I came in?' he asked from outside, as if for all the world he had never seen her naked, never walked into her bathroom. Or perhaps he was just being obedient.

'Don't be silly, Devlin,' she said with no malice.

He came into the bathroom with the air of a schoolboy entering the headmaster's study after being caught in some particularly heinous crime by the senior prefect. Stephanie had to laugh.

'Oh Devlin. Come and sit by the bath,' she said, indicating the marble ledge. 'Don't look so apprehensive. I'm not going to bite.'

He sat down gingerly, his buttocks clearly still feeling the effects of the beating.

'I thought we should have a serious talk.'

'Pour yourself a glass of champagne. And fill mine.'

He did as he was told.

'Would you rather I came back . . .' He found her naked body distracting.

'Devlin, say what you've got to say. It's a bit late for false modesty, isn't it?'

Her breasts seemed to be floating in the water. He could see the line of her body clearly, the dark patch of her pubic hair disappearing down between her legs. He tried to concentrate. Much to his surprise he felt his cock stirring in his trousers, an experience that was quite new to him. It reinforced his determination to say what he had come to say.

'First I want to apologise. This whole thing with Gianni. You must believe me, it came up so suddenly. I didn't bring you here for his benefit. I swear. Nothing could have been further from my mind.'

'You let him use me.'

'Yes. I was desperate. My whole business was on the line. All this. Everything. If he'd walked away without signing the deal. And after meeting you he just refused to do the deal. What else could I do? I suppose I've got used to using the castle as a way of persuading people to my point of view. Usually people are only too happy to indulge themselves in the cellars and then come to an amicable arrangement over business matters. Gianni just wasn't interested. He only wanted you. Nevertheless I shouldn't have let it happen.'

For a moment Stephanie said nothing. It was not that

208

Stephanie did not know what she was going to say but she thought she should keep Devlin in suspense a moment longer.

'Apology accepted,' she said finally. 'What else?'

'You mean it?' He looked ecstatic.

'I don't say things I don't mean, Devlin,' she said allowing a stern note to creep back into her voice.

'You don't know how much that means to me, my dear. You really are an extraordinary woman.'

'That's not all though, is it?' Stephanie knew Devlin had not finished. The apology was only a prelude.

'No.'

'Spit it out then,' she said running a little more hot water into the tub and taking another sip of the fine champagne.

'This morning . . .'

'Yes?' she prompted.

'I just wanted to tell you . . .' he paused again.

'Devlin, say it,' she said impatiently.

'I just wanted to say, Stephanie, that it was the most exciting experience of my life. Ever.'

'Good,' she said knowing there was still more to come.

Devlin took a deep breath.

'It's just that . . . Well I've been thinking. Now Gianni's taken the property off my hands, well, everything's back on an even keel. I mean, I'm never going to make that mistake again, I promise you. I just got greedy. A bridge too far. So, well . . .' He paused for a third time but Stephanie said nothing. 'I've never known a woman like you. You're so lovely. So strong. You have this incredible sexuality, why don't you come here, run the castle for me? Run the slaves. The castle needs someone like you. Someone with real imagination. You're so good at it. On your own terms of course. Whatever you want. You can have anything you want.'

'Well, you have done a lot of thinking, haven't you?'

'It's what this place needs. We can really make it work. I've never used it properly. You have this ability to know what people want. It's like a gift, an instinct you have. We need you here, Stephanie. I need you here.'

He was right. Stephanie knew he was right. Everything he said rang true to her. Everything he said she had thought herself over the last two days, since he had first taken her down into the cellars. Devlin had created an extraordinary resource but it was not being used to its full potential. Stephanie knew she could change that.

'And of course,' Devlin said sheepishly, 'when I can get away from running the business . . .'

'Yes?'

'I would . . .'

'Say it, Devlin,' Stephanie said sternly.

'I would want to be one of your slaves too.'

She laughed and got up out of the bath, the water running off her body. The water ran down into her thick pubic hair which funnelled it into a single stream running off her body between her legs. It looked as if she was peeing.

'Would you now.' She used his shoulder to steady herself as she stepped out of the bathtub then handed him a towel. 'Dry me then. At least you're good at that.'

He immediately set to work as before, rubbing and patting her dry in a purely utilitarian way. Neither of them spoke. Stephanie was thinking of his offer. Devlin was amazed that even this non-sexual activity had caused his penis to stir to erection again. Whatever effect Stephanie had had on him it seemed to be permanent.

When he was finished she walked through into the bedroom. She found the more functional of her two swimsuits and stepped into it, pulling it up her body and slipping the straps over her shoulders. Devlin watched as she adjusted the elastic between her legs and eased the material, better to accommodate her breasts.

'I thought I'd take the motorboat out on the lake. It's such a beautiful afternoon,' she said. 'Will you come?'

'I'd love to.'

'Good.'

'And my offer?'

'I'll think about it.'

'Oh, come on, don't keep me in suspense.' It was the voice of the old Devlin, the confident powerful businessman annoyed at a minor colleague's behaviour, not the anxious voice of the humble and humbled slave.

'What did you say?' For some reason, unconscious no doubt, Stephanie had brought the riding crop up from the cellars. It was lying on the bed and she picked it up. 'What did you say?'

'I meant you can give me your answer whenever you like. Whenever ...' he mumbled watching the tip of the crop and feeling anew the soreness of his arse.

'Whenever *I* like?' she emphasised.

'Whenever *you* like,' Devlin repeated obediently.

Stephanie raised the rising crop. She used the thick leather loop at its tip to stroke Devlin's cheek. He made no attempt to move. Then she noticed the large bulge protruding from the front of his trousers. She prodded it with the whip.

'Well, what have we here?'

'My erection,' he said quietly, his head bowed.

'There was a time when you found it very difficult to get spontaneous erections, wasn't there?'

'Yes.'

'So what's happened?'

'You,' he said simply.

She hooked the leather under his chin and made him raise his head.

'Look at me, Devlin,' she ordered.

He looked into her eyes as the leather crop pressed into

the flesh of his throat. Stephanie could see a flicker of fear in his eyes but it was combined, she could see clearly, with a look of hungry anticipation. This was new territory for him. He wanted more. The master had become the slave.

Stephanie was in no rush to make her decision. Before dinner on Sunday night she called her boss at his home in London and told him she wasn't feeling well and wouldn't be in on Monday and maybe not Tuesday either (she didn't add, or ever again). Even though she hadn't bothered to use an ill-sounding voice he sympathised with her and hoped she would get well soon. As she was speaking she had a sudden image of him – he was seriously overweight with a paunch the size of a pregnant woman – bent over one of the punishment frames in the cellars, his naked arse striped with marks from the crop, popped into her head. She had to work hard to suppress the sound of amusement in her voice.

She spent a great deal of time getting ready for dinner, deciding to wear a strapless number she had spotted in the next-door wardrobe when she had been searching through them with Colette. The lemon yellow suited her black hair and though it clung to her body like a glove the material was thick nobbly silk. She wore stockings and her highest heels.

At her request she'd asked Devlin for Venetia to join them at dinner. So Devlin sat, at the glass-topped table, between two women, a sumptuous blonde and an elegant brunette. Venetia was wearing black, a halter-necked dress that left her back completely naked and made it impossible for her to wear a bra. Both women had tied their hair up.

Devlin was charm itself, attending to their every wish and treating Venetia as an equal. Clearly he was anxious to hear Stephanie's answer but did not prompt her in any way. And, of course, there was still the unfinished business to deal with.

'The masked slave, Devlin. When does he go back?'

'The early flight tomorrow.'

'Well, that only leaves tonight then,' Stephanie mused.

'What do you mean?' Devlin asked tentatively.

'Devlin, you can't possibly imagine he is not going to have to pay for what he did to Venetia?'

'Oh . . .' was all Devlin could think of saying. It would be pointless to defend the man.

'And Devlin, there's something else I want from you.'

'I told you, you can have anything.'

'Venetia and I will be paying Gianni a visit tomorrow. Not a visit I think he will enjoy. You will arrange it. Make sure he's at home. I'm sure you can do that. Naturally we want to make it a surprise so you'll have to think of some excuse to keep him in.'

'I'll certainly do that,' Devlin said smiling. The thought of Gianni being made to suffer was something that delighted him. And it would do no harm to remind him of his visit to the cellars. He felt sure, after Stephanie's visit, that after his 'punishment' Gianni might well want to return to them again quite soon, and that would be helpful in future business transactions. After the way Gianni had behaved this weekend Devlin would have no compunction in exploiting any advantage over him.

'Where is he based?' Stephanie asked.

'Rome.'

'Oh, well, we can do some shopping while we're there, can't we? A stroll down the Via Veneto.'

'I'll have it all arranged.'

'Perfect,' Stephanie said.

At the end of the meal Stephanie got up and took Venetia's hand.

'Come on, we've got work to do.' They headed for the

door, then Stephanie paused. 'And when we get back from Rome I'll give you my decision, Devlin.'

'Thank you. Ah, Stephanie . . .' Devlin hesitated.

'Yes?'

'Can I come and watch?'

'Can I come and watch. I think you better ask properly if you want something in future, don't you, Devlin?' Stephanie said in her sternest voice.

'Can I come and watch, mistress?' Devlin said quietly.

'That's better. Remember it.'

'Can I, mistress?'

'Yes.'

Stephanie strode down to the cellars, Venetia and Devlin following in her wake. Later that night she wanted to lie with Venetia, feel that long soft body next to hers again, caress and be caressed, use and be used. But first things had to come first.

The masked man dropped to his knees in the prescribed position as soon as Bruno unlocked the cell door. He was still wearing the tight black mask he had worn the night before. He was not surprised to see the two women walk into his cell though he had no reason to expect it. The two women in their fine couture evening dresses, elegant shoes and sheer hosiery contrasted starkly with the stone walls and floor of the cell and the thin stained material of the mattress. The scene looked like an outré set-up for a fashion photographer with Stephanie and Venetia modelling the latest evening wear.

'The question is,' Stephanie said, 'what exactly are we going to do with you?'

Devlin shuffled into the cell. Whatever had happened since last night, when Devlin had been giving the orders, it was quite clear from his whole posture and attitude that he was in no position now to command or interfere with anything. He was here as a spectator.

Nor was it difficult to work out who was in control. The masked man could see it in the way the woman from the plane, he did not know her name, stood and from the way her whole presence exuded an air of authority. He had seen it on the plane when the stewardess had challenged her, seen her ability to take charge: but now her power seemed to have grown. Her confidence was absolute, her assurance complete.

'I think we should make the punishment fit the crime. Some sort of poetic justice.'

Stephanie unhooked the halter of the black dress from Venetia's neck so the front fell away to reveal her large plump breasts. Stephanie stroked them both, taking each in turn to feel its weight.

'Beautiful, aren't they?' The man in the mask nodded, as the question was clearly addressed to him.

Stephanie unzipped the skirt of the dress at the back so that it too fell away. Venetia stepped out of it and stood in only a pair of high-cut black satin knickers pulled tight on to her hips and sheer black hold-up stockings, spun with Lycra to make them shiny and slippery-looking, her high heels shaping her calves and thighs in sculptured curves.

The masked man's penis pushed hopelessly against the hard leather pouch trying to come to erection but cruelly restrained. His balls and cock were in agony. The more his excitement grew the greater the hurt. The pressure made it impossible for him to stand up straight, and he crouched, trying to ease the pain.

'So as you gave Venetia an experience she hadn't had before, it only seems fair that she should do the same to you.' Stephanie's voice was hard and callous.

The man knew immediately what she meant. As Venetia left the cell he knew precisely what she was going to fetch. He wanted to explain that he was only obeying orders, that it was Devlin's fault, that he had no choice but the gag prevented him. He tried to say it with his eyes and ask for mercy. But he knew, even if he could have pleaded his case it would have done no good. Not with this woman. She was implacable, her eyes sparkling, her enjoyment obvious. There was nothing that would change her mind.

Stephanie smiled to herself as she waited for Venetia to return. She had no intention of telling Devlin yet, but in her own mind Stephanie had made her decision. In fact, she had made it moments after Devlin made his offer. It was the obvious extension of everything she had felt and experienced over the last three days. Her life had changed. There was a lot to be done, a lot to work out. She was going to make sure Devlin never got into another mess like the situation with Gianni. She would become the mistress of the castle, and, though he did not know it yet, the mistress of a great deal more. She would insinuate her way into his business and his life. Devlin's castle would become hers. Her castle. Stephanie's castle.

Nexus

NEXUS BACKLIST

All books are priced £4.99 unless another price is given. If a date is supplied, the book in question will not be available until that month in 1995.

CONTEMPORARY EROTICA

THE ACADEMY	Arabella Knight	
CONDUCT UNBECOMING	Arabella Knight	Jul
CONTOURS OF DARKNESS	Marco Vassi	
THE DEVIL'S ADVOCATE	Anonymous	
DIFFERENT STROKES	Sarah Veitch	Aug
THE DOMINO TATTOO	Cyrian Amberlake	
THE DOMINO ENIGMA	Cyrian Amberlake	
THE DOMINO QUEEN	Cyrian Amberlake	
ELAINE	Stephen Ferris	
EMMA'S SECRET WORLD	Hilary James	
EMMA ENSLAVED	Hilary James	
EMMA'S SECRET DIARIES	Hilary James	
FALLEN ANGELS	Kendal Grahame	
THE FANTASIES OF JOSEPHINE SCOTT	Josephine Scott	
THE GENTLE DEGENERATES	Marco Vassi	
HEART OF DESIRE	Maria del Rey	
HELEN – A MODERN ODALISQUE	Larry Stern	
HIS MISTRESS'S VOICE	G. C. Scott	
HOUSE OF ANGELS	Yvonne Strickland	May
THE HOUSE OF MALDONA	Yolanda Celbridge	
THE IMAGE	Jean de Berg	Jul
THE INSTITUTE	Maria del Rey	
SISTERHOOD OF THE INSTITUTE	Maria del Rey	

Title	Author	Month
JENNIFER'S INSTRUCTION	Cyrian Amberlake	
LETTERS TO CHLOE	Stefan Gerrard	Aug
LINGERING LESSONS	Sarah Veitch	Apr
A MATTER OF POSSESSION	G. C. Scott	Sep
MELINDA AND THE MASTER	Susanna Hughes	
MELINDA AND ESMERALDA	Susanna Hughes	
MELINDA AND THE COUNTESS	Susanna Hughes	
MELINDA AND THE ROMAN	Susanna Hughes	
MIND BLOWER	Marco Vassi	
MS DEEDES ON PARADISE ISLAND	Carole Andrews	
THE NEW STORY OF O	Anonymous	
OBSESSION	Maria del Rey	
ONE WEEK IN THE PRIVATE HOUSE	Esme Ombreux	Jun
THE PALACE OF SWEETHEARTS	Delver Maddingley	
THE PALACE OF FANTASIES	Delver Maddingley	
THE PALACE OF HONEYMOONS	Delver Maddingley	
THE PALACE OF EROS	Delver Maddingley	
PARADISE BAY	Maria del Rey	
THE PASSIVE VOICE	G. C. Scott	
THE SALINE SOLUTION	Marco Vassi	
SHERRIE	Evelyn Culber	May
STEPHANIE	Susanna Hughes	
STEPHANIE'S CASTLE	Susanna Hughes	
STEPHANIE'S REVENGE	Susanna Hughes	
STEPHANIE'S DOMAIN	Susanna Hughes	
STEPHANIE'S TRIAL	Susanna Hughes	
STEPHANIE'S PLEASURE	Susanna Hughes	
THE TEACHING OF FAITH	Elizabeth Bruce	
THE TRAINING GROUNDS	Sarah Veitch	
UNDERWORLD	Maria del Rey	

EROTIC SCIENCE FICTION

Title	Author	Month
ADVENTURES IN THE PLEASUREZONE	Delaney Silver	
RETURN TO THE PLEASUREZONE	Delaney Silver	

FANTASYWORLD	Larry Stern	
WANTON	Andrea Arven	

ANCIENT & FANTASY SETTINGS

CHAMPIONS OF LOVE	Anonymous	
CHAMPIONS OF PLEASURE	Anonymous	
CHAMPIONS OF DESIRE	Anonymous	
THE CLOAK OF APHRODITE	Kendal Grahame	
THE HANDMAIDENS	Aran Ashe	
THE SLAVE OF LIDIR	Aran Ashe	
THE DUNGEONS OF LIDIR	Aran Ashe	
THE FOREST OF BONDAGE	Aran Ashe	
PLEASURE ISLAND	Aran Ashe	
WITCH QUEEN OF VIXANIA	Morgana Baron	

EDWARDIAN, VICTORIAN & OLDER EROTICA

ANNIE	Evelyn Culber	
ANNIE AND THE SOCIETY	Evelyn Culber	
THE AWAKENING OF LYDIA	Philippa Masters	Apr
BEATRICE	Anonymous	
CHOOSING LOVERS FOR JUSTINE	Aran Ashe	
GARDENS OF DESIRE	Roger Rougiere	
THE LASCIVIOUS MONK	Anonymous	
LURE OF THE MANOR	Barbra Baron	
RETURN TO THE MANOR	Barbra Baron	Jun
MAN WITH A MAID 1	Anonymous	
MAN WITH A MAID 2	Anonymous	
MAN WITH A MAID 3	Anonymous	
MEMOIRS OF A CORNISH GOVERNESS	Yolanda Celbridge	
THE GOVERNESS AT ST AGATHA'S	Yolanda Celbridge	
TIME OF HER LIFE	Josephine Scott	
VIOLETTE	Anonymous	

THE JAZZ AGE

BLUE ANGEL NIGHTS	Margarete von Falkensee	
BLUE ANGEL DAYS	Margarete von Falkensee	

Please send me the books I have ticked above.

Name ....

Address ....

....

....

.... Post code ....

Send to: **Cash Sales, Nexus Books, 332 Ladbroke Grove, London W10 5AH.**

Please enclose a cheque or postal order, made payable to **Nexus Books**, to the value of the books you have ordered plus postage and packing costs as follows:

UK and BFPO – £1.00 for the first book, 50p for each subsequent book.

Overseas (including Republic of Ireland) – £2.00 for the first book, £1.00 for the second book, and 50p for each subsequent book.

If you would prefer to pay by VISA or ACCESS/MASTERCARD, please write your card number and expiry date here:

....

Please allow up to 28 days for delivery.

Signature ....